A Reflection

2 Corinthians 1:3-5

James 1:22-25

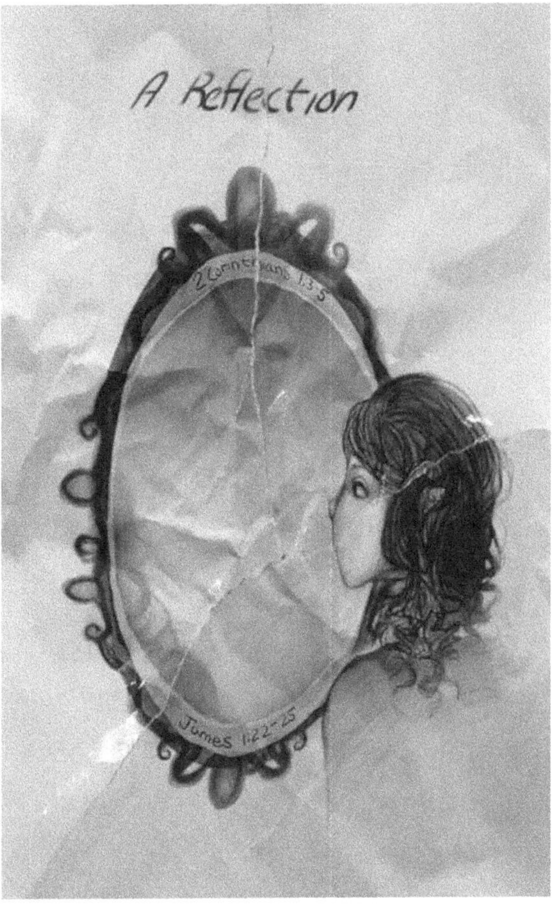

Christiamity

A Reflection

Price Obot

No Frills
<<<>>>
Buffalo

Printed in the United States of America

Obot, Price

Christiamity/Obot- 1st Edition

ISBN: 978-0615725673

1. Christiamity – Fiction.   2. New Author – No Frills. 3. Christian
Fiction
1. Title

No Frills Buffalo Press
119 Dorchester Buffalo, New York 14213
For More Information Visit Nofrillsbuffalo.com

My gratitude to the following:

Zoe Yera

Special thanks:

Sarah Dewasmes Obot

Christiamity

A Reflection

Dream Work

Vibration. It repeats and gains attention. A sound that of flushing, and lasting a few seconds less than its reason. A body feels and forms, feminine in undergarments and female in shape. Strolling through house halls with a grip, the phone. Sharp is the conversation sensed not heard, felt but not understood. There was no goal to the course, just a stop to listen, pay attention:

She's going off to Rochester come September.

Yeah, Ethel and I can't wait to see her off.

That's beautiful, she's a great girl.

You know what she's studying?

Something about media, right John?

Media Studies.

Oh, that's right.

Well, you don't let her go without holding her tight, 'cause once she's gone, you see her when she wants to be seen. Ask Happi here.

Yep. Our Maddie only came up a few times this year, and barely a couple last year.

But we understand she's busy, after all, her parents pay a lot of money to have her go to that school, so they better keep her busy.

That sound of pleasant laughter, ill, was well known. Visitors were less so, familiar somehow, and foreign all together. Again, vibrations go, this time, unnoticed.

Busy? Well, that's what she tells us. God knows what she's busy *doing down there. For all I know she could say one thing, and be* doing *another.*

Happi, you know she wouldn't lie to us.

She wouldn't? She doesn't have to. You happen to believe everything she says. You've seen the way she's on her phone the few times she's here, haven't you? What is she doing, school work? You've heard the way she talks, and that one has been around since high school. And you had to have seen the way she dresses, I mean she must not think she is a girl because she's like a woman now, and a first class...

Happi! She's not a little girl anymore. Don't you see that*? She may just be experimenting, and finding out who she really is, and you know she's not what you're making her out to be.*

Oh no, Ben. You're not the only one who's been paying attention. What slipped by your monitor is that she is no longer a little girl. That like her mother she...

      Happi...

No, Ethel, he has to hear this. Your Maddie is no longer your little girl because she's no longer even a virgin.

Happi, how can you say that? How can you even think that she...

Ben, the truth is I don't think it was just once, nor...

Happiness... I can't... brith...

Vibrations, now with all attention, were attended, an audience of one and three observers. Staggered eyes, observant of the undergarment body. The fifth, his right arm hugging his body, barely noticed, gasped for air. Awkwardly, to a rippling floor, fifth falls. Happiness, lack thereof, causes and maintains, three times over, his death.

See? See, see?

Burning, tearing, melting, the female face dissolves. Vibrations continue. Senses awaken, and as the sleep dies, the dream slumbers but lives. Usually a beautiful girl, Memory was that morning unhappy and ugly. Somewhere, there awoke a groggy mind to a buzzing cellular device, "what Frank," voiced that soul, "why," and upon some answer, reposed. "Bye."

Un

Summer in Western New York, at last, was less a relief to most, and more an expected due for the finally melted snow and disappearance of blue-gray skies. Imaginably, there were expectations for weather, and after coming out of yet another Buffalo winter, whose reputation was more infamous for its denizens than famous, the usual short spring was expected. However, as students in Western New York colleges remember, showers came at a time when there were to be flowers. Not in April, but May.

Although, admittedly, this made for beautifully contrasted greens with dark browns in the fore of gray-blue skies, it prevented certain students from participating in outdoor activities as they would like them. It hampered the exploration of new environments on campuses and brought an overall protraction of weather doldrums that began, seemingly, much too long before during the winter.

With greater frequency in the visitation of the sun's rays upon grounds, and length with respect to their duration, there was more than kinetic increase which resulted in heat. Seemingly, there was a correlation between the nascent summer and the increase in activity on the campus. Any observer with some faculty of senses could observe in the youth about on bikes, skateboards, and other means of moving about, the coming of the much awaited summer. Impromptu games of Frisbee, soccer, and football were also telling of the change in atmosphere, both physically and psychologically. This was summer, on, at Canisius College.

The arrival of the summer meant nothing more than a change in weather for the academic institution, for teaching and instruction continued for many, and campus activity may have diminished, but remained at some constant threshold. For others there were internships to fulfill and work in which to engage. Specifically, yet for some, summer represented the beginning of research or classes, both, or even greater engagement in reading or writing. This was the case for some healthcare-oriented students, or so it would seem, who enrolled in the Social and Ethical Values in Medicine course offered during the summer sessions at Canisius. For these students, given the choice, they had opted to give a part of their summer, perhaps, to fulfill a requirement of their studies in choosing to take the course.

It was much different. The walkways, lecture halls, dining areas, and recognizable scenes of the institution, that is. Exiting the REWSC, or Richard E. Winter Student Center as it were, the antechamber-like area that could serve as a lobby to the REWSC had within it students dispersed throughout on computer-laptops, engaged with books or enjoying conversations on mobile devices. Passing through and under the many bridges and archways, apparent was the decreased frequency in vehicles or busses and the students that stepped out of them. Contrast this with the usual occurrence in which students would spill out of busses as though they were onboard mobile classrooms whose duration was determined by the length of spaces between stops. But this was because a majority of observable students were enjoying the sun, benches were occupied with readers and texters alike, walking seemed the most popular means of getting around, and in passing the outdoor tables, one could hear snippets of conversation not unlike, "… should like… in Dr. Garret's… group?" Truthfully, to the new students on campus, perhaps, the activity level and immediate Canisius population was dwindled and perhaps even painfully boring. But in reality, hidden and tucked in corners, certain halls and classrooms, were intense concentrations of students participating in research and, in the case of that Philosophy course already mentioned, classes that had more to do with real life than the philosophy behind the fundamental and general concepts that science found unwieldy.

~

Directly west of the REWSC, but slightly to its south, is a parking lot seemingly too small to hold as many cars as its spaces suggest. Simultaneously serving as a parking space for the academic halls of Bouwhuis and Science, to which it is closest, it almost certainly is not uncommon that people park there even when they are not science-oriented students. This occurrence is not specific to Main-Jefferson lot, and in fact, it could be argued this happens campus wide. Main-Jefferson is the last parking lot at the end of Hughes Avenue, which originates near the Humboldt Parkway, and having access to the "caniche hoods" as given by Meech Avenue near its middle section, ends at Jefferson Avenue, but not before serving the REWSC. From the lot, proximally, visible is the CAT, or Churchill Academic Tower, of which only the top of its cylinder upon cylinder structure can be seen as it is the background to the aforementioned Bouwhuis Library. With the Bouwhuis to its south, the CAT is surrounded by three buildings; Old Main to its east and the Bagen Administration Building to its north circumference. More distant, are the Tech Center and Cultural Center which can barely be made out from the lot as their viewing from the vantage can only be partial. And across from these, as Main Street bisects the Main campus, is the Commons. Something of a medley of buildings with a dim sum of purposes.

Housed on the first of several floors are many restaurants whose diversity intelligently reflects that of the college population, and although a few boutiques hold their own on this level, it is almost a certainty that students who frequent the first floor are attending either a fast-food or dining restaurant. Whether African-American, Caucasian, Indian or Chinese, there was something to please the palate at these restaurants, and purportedly, the Chinese "place" was popular for reasons including flavor, and greater "bang for buck", which is certainly important given the dearth of money. This is the Commons. What serves as a courtyard is a small open area in which there are walkways leading from the entrances of the fronts to the restaurants in the rear of the Commons. The more prominent features, however, are few dispersed trees, two symmetric square fountains which Canadian geese and even canard frequent, and a structure in the front of Lyons Hall. A lattice-work structure that resembles the framework of an unfinished mini-skyscraper is a defining component of the Common's courtyard, for atop the structure, held, is a house-like pinnacle with its four walls holding a clock, which would seem to remind of London. For one reason—balconies—or another, apartment-like windows, the upper levels resemble apartment complexes, living quarters, or living areas. Adding to this falsity, perhaps, is the frequency with which "older" looking students are about the upper levels, which consists the second and third floors. But, in fact, the upper levels are almost entirely the graduate student associations, and sense was found in connecting these upper levels with each other, utilizing the underground passageways and other such enclosed corridors.

These are all visible from the Main-Jefferson lot given its central locale to these locations. In a small way the interconnectivity of the College can be seen, and while this is a component of Canisius efficiency, it is minor as this is certainly true of other colleges and universities as well. However, the last of the major objects, in buildings, that is observable from Main-Jefferson, is the Science Hall which eclipses much of the southern view from the lot. Seemingly unimportant in the milieu of other academic halls, it certainly, in the way of significance, held nothing for the PHI 337 students other than containing the classroom in which the course would be conducted. But it was in *this* hall, somewhere among its many classrooms, that part of an interesting story, although not terribly exciting, would take place. It was the summer of 2014, the 8th of July.

Deux

July was a particularly exciting time for students as it held in time the full anticipation of summer, research or classes, especially for those whose first year had elapsed at Canisius. With final grades and marks already meted, along with the possibilities in catching up with erstwhile friends to boot, this confluence of circumstances along with spending more time with family, and as such in a greater capacity, was simply exciting. And this was not less true for two students in particular. The first, a young woman, being a chemistry major whose first year at the College had come to a close. The undergraduate had brains to complement her pretty, and although she had her interests and now knew them fairly well, had experienced difficulties during her first and second semesters, most of which could be attributed to relatively recent family problems. At the time, she was in a relationship with which she could have been less excited, and was enrolled in the summer class less out of volition and more because of necessity.

There, on the first day of classes, drove a green hatchback automobile into Main-Jefferson and filled a space as close to the Science Hall as was possible. The vehicle was of the Ford make, it was tennis-shoe-like with contrasting yellow signal-lights in the front and red tail-lights that hugged the rear of the vehicle just below a spoiler, and at times stalled for seemingly no reason. With only two doors along with its hatchback, the car was small and compact, much like its driver. As she stepped out of her car, it was clear that the girl was admirable, neither too tall nor very short. Choosing a skirt over pants, her exposed legs were toned, telling of her history of movement in physical activity. Her feet were uncovered but crossed about by two strips of material that emerged between her pollux and juxtaposed toe, and ran medially and laterally, each, to join the flatness that flipped and flopped as she departed from her car. Directing her not toward Science, but toward the on-campus café in the Commons. The pedicure of her toes, however lacking nail polish, indicated she was particular to certain things but not others. In example, given the fairly warm and bright day, her decision to don a skirt versus pants but not to wear sunglasses in that almost girly chic fashion of that day, with big rims and large temple arms, was a result of her personality and attitude, for she could just as easily pierce her nose, but refuse to wear earrings. In fact, that is what she did.

Her gait was marked by a posture that set apart her legs just enough to give her hips credit in their width, and as such the tight material about her waist that held the breezy, but short, black skirt in place simultaneously served as a rough indicator of the middle of her hourglass figure. Her sway would have the rear rise and fall independently and oppositely giving her a characteristic chic influence, but given her low self-monitoring, this she would have denied as a falsity. The blouse was revealing but not tight, giving way to her breasts which otherwise would have been deceivingly smaller and hiding toned abdominals which, admittedly, had been added to, along with the midsection of her rear as well, by adiposities. This, more or less, added to the suppleness of her otherwise hard frame. But it is not in these aspects that her attitude, nor personality, could be captured, for her demeanor, not her posture, was most telling. The piercing of her nose aside, her countenance was given by rouge-aided lips that parted slightly on every breath and, sharply contrasting, by the brunette of her hair which twisted and curled as though from root to end their lengths were the reptilian bodies of snakes. Well done was her makeup and its fineness reflected in the lack of pallor to her face. And it was the black tines of her eyelashes along with the crypts of Fuch, which gave her iris a silver-blue color, that gave her a look that could seemingly cut through what and those she regarded, but not before incapacitating them as if turned to stone by Medusa herself. Or so she liked to think.

She did as she pleased and often would for she was impulsive, though this was perhaps due to low ego-control, and had a hard and rebellious nature she often characterized as "bad-ass." She entered and closed the door to the café as she observed the bright of the outside diminish to the kitchen-like glow of the inside. The immediacy of her slight introversion was evident in her avoidance of others. Or, perhaps, this was a result of her slight neuroticism in that she feared, however slightly, that looking on others unwarrantedly would result in an accosting she ironically would put much energy into winning. It was not without her many idiosyncrasies to have a black and white nature. In fact, she was full of contradictions, and as such it is no surprise that her distaste for carbonated beverages was contrasted by her eager taste for lime diet-coke. In addition, her disgust for sticky and sugary foods would have excluded peanut butter, certain cheeses, caramel, and tart, cherry filling from her palate but with the exception of cherry-pie and caramel when it was presented in a coffee beverage, as this was among her favorite of beverages. Considerably, she was a character in herself. It would not have been unexpected to find juxtaposed to her Madeline Welsch of a name, "badass," as though it were an integral part of her name, and so person, though it certainly was in her personality.

"I'll have a frappuccino," she commanded the tall, dark-haired cashier.

Pushing up his glasses, "would you like caramel in that," asked the male.

"Of course," she smirked, "but without the topping." He smiled at her, and though she was only nineteen the cashier would have guessed incorrectly.

~

In some of the campus buildings there are laboratory settings in which simple to complex laboratory procedures, education, and training take place. One such building is the Hoods, or Horan-O'Donnell Science Building, which is similar to the Health (Health

Sciences) Building in purpose, but not in design. During the regular semesters it is common to see students, undergraduate and graduate alike, frequenting the two buildings. Some about their studies, others about their lives and future as the life of graduate students is often inseparable from the lab or their academic obligations in general. It is, however, uncommon to have research, or any training for that matter, conducted on the campus during the summer. The majority of laboratory setting practices are relegated to the South Medical Campus buildings which are a fairly straight ten- or less minute drive down the trite Main Street. As such, if one makes their way through the halls of the South Medical Campus, the likes of Fary or Carber, they will find in observation the emptiness of the halls which are often narrow. Perhaps allowing for roomier labs which often seem to contain more equipment and persons than could be within their capacity. It would follow logic, however, that most occupants of Medical South do little to frequent the long narrow halls and much to attend the multitude of whatever it is that keeps their attention captive in capacious rooms.

Was it true that without the online campus information and other such news about ongoing matters at the College that some students, and even faculty, would not have been aware of the changes in weather? No, ostensibly, of course not. But it must be understood that Canisius is an intensely research-focused institution, however academic. This meant more than students and faculty alike spending much of their time in laboratories and lecture halls.

"These lab hours are killing me," said a nondescript voice behind a Fary Hall door to the lab room 3A. The voice, although that of youth, had to it a timbre of wisdom, as if given by age, and a course smoothness not unlike a slushee.

"Yeah," the second voice drew out with the tail-end of a sigh, "not that I don't appreciate all you've shown me today, but," there was an airy quality to this sound which was given by a playful nature and in no way did away with the sex-specific tone indicative of a male, "there's a time for everything, and it is time for me to get out of here."

Directly in front of the door were a set of instruments and laboratory equipment that could frighten laboratory animals as well as dismay novice and inexperienced students. With variable sized tubes, some interconnected and others white islands of their own in a black sea that was the table top, containers, and other such instruments in no particular order but having some organization with respect to their purposes in and about the room, the only space available to the two students were the small tables whose limited spaces were crowded with desktop computers.

"Now I'm never sure if or when you're making jest and when you're making a biblical reference," responded the young gentleman whose French origin was not given away by an accent. Asking, "but you begin classes today don't you?"

The former was a graduate student in the biological sciences working toward a master's degree, and the latter, "yep, that's actually why I gotta go, I want to prepare and get some reading done and everything, you know," an undergraduate student who was busy enough in studies and laboratory not to realize he had but finished his first semester at the College. Preparing his bag in a particular way, the undergraduate inserted the school newspaper into a zipper portion of the bag as he gave his goodbye, "see you next week Gustav," and Gustav nodded in response.

As he took the second corner to the room from which he came, he saw a sign that was all too familiar. It read, "Dr. Pfordresher," with an arrow pointing out the way toward the lab. It was this very sign that he had followed to make his initial meeting with the professor of biomedical sciences in whose lab he currently was a research assistant, and so it made sense that he, in passing, was reminded of his efforts which had gained him experience as a first-year student. The halls were long, they were narrow, lined with many doors to many labs, and were in some way interconnected. But to this, as in many things, there was an exception. Staring down that exception, he could see the many doors that sealed off the offices to some important people he did not know, and as he walked, observable were the electronic displays of messages contained in the squared-off organic, light-emitting diodes of a screen with information ranging from weather to current events and campus news. The message boards, which seemed to copy the marbled floors when they were filled, along with name plates which seemed the caption of all the displays were but on the sidelines to what was the center of focus, however. At the head of the main hall, as it were, which simultaneously served as the main entrance to Carber Hall, was held, as if in free captivity, a predatory animal of mosaic composition that very much resembled the actual beast. But only in size. The griffin was clad in multiple colors which, each surrounding small lettered words or phrases that had much if not all to do with medicine, gave it texture. Paradoxically, he thought, though the words were small, some quite short, he knew people to think them "big" words, and although he knew many of them it was unlikely as much for a graduate student as for him to know a majority or all of them. In his usual routine, he stopped to read a new word. "Concomitant," he read. Knowing many of the words, including concomitance, he wanted to know a lot more of them, and truth be told, he wanted to know all of them.

Outside, the din of the bus was less a croak and more a discordant rhythmic protest of air in the engine. Students and passengers, for who could discriminate, strode on in a more leisure manner for it was summer, it was bright outside and no one was rushing in to escape the drear or the cold. The last student-passenger to get on was an undergraduate who wore darker-than-navy-blue shorts, tan flip flops, and a light blue polo shirt. He would have preferred the blue and gold bags of the College that carried its logo, a griffin, but his studies and activities required he have a backpack. Brushing off the straps to the pack, he shed its weight off his shoulders and onto the seat adjacent to the one he placed himself. The rays that caused short shadows in the cabin gave his cranium a coarse reflection, for his head was not bald but had little hair. His skin was darker than reservoir red which was the color it reflected of the sun's bright yellow, it seemed to have its own glow given its smoothness. Being one of few who did not find a need to use electronic devices to help pass time during the short bus ride, he began tapping a beat with his feet as his head bobbed in rhythm, oscillating to find a face at which he could smile or pose a pleasant look. It could be said that he was extraverted for that was a fairly accurate description of his personality at times, and at others less so; his self control was enough at times to still him which helped his faculties in judgment, but it incapacitated him, some could argue, in moments of action or decision.

Taking the final turn onto Main which would lead straight, more or less, to the Main campus, the bus made a wide right turn. As most of the bodies swayed towards the driver side of the bus, there was a female student who confirmed her suspicions of the black passenger whose gaze was at times directed at her, and whose attention was not unwelcomed, but just unusual. She was unsure if it was his seemingly positive demeanor or the complementary blue of his blouse that was so much to her liking.

She was not surprised when he accosted her, "I see you have an orgo chem book, what is your major?" The mutual empathy between students of the sciences was evident even in the beginning of the exchange, and when it came to organic chemistry there was a greater feel of togetherness.

"Oh," looking at the books and notebooks in her lap, "this, I, I'm a pharmacy major," she answered, "most of my classes are on the Main," referring to the main campus. "But I have lab, for some reason, on Medical South" she continued and, herself feeling more confident, posed, "and you?"

He was not muscled but toned, his personality complemented his face which had the ability to smile without showing teeth, and his character could be detected in his posture, erect, held up and well angled. "I'm a bio major," he answered, "I go down to Medical South for labs as well, but fortunately I don't have to carry any books, just folders."

"What class do you have lab, especially since you don't carry books, 'just folders'," she joked, smiling.

Her jest did not warrant such amusement, but he responded in kind by smiling in return, then sobering as he made his point, "oh, it's not a class, the lab is not for class but research," he added for the purpose of clarification. "I'm an RA."

Understanding, or so it seemed given her bright response with lifted eyebrows, wide eyes and open mouth, "nice, but that means you must go to Medical South often."

The bus was entering the semi-loop in which it would soon empty momentarily before being more or less filled by south-bound students. The passengers were aware of this and began, one by one, standing as the bus bypassed cars parked by the side of the loop and heading toward its head. As he got up, he gave his response with Gustav in mind, "au contraire, actually I go down about two or three times a week, which is great especially considering gas what it is now in prices."

She nodded in understanding as she too made her way up. The hanging plastic handles or grip-holds swayed just above their heads as the bus slowed to stop as it simultaneously turned to avoid the curvilinear curb. He was sure to watch his head in order to avoid the swinging grip-holds, tall enough that they bothered him but not so much that he towered over his temporary companion. "That must be exciting, isn't it, I can't wait until I'm accepted into a lab," she expressed, "but I'm also sure there is a lot of work."

Looking to be sure of footing while making their way off the bus, the two had final exchanges, "you're correct both times, and long story short, read," he said, adding, "hey, you have a good day."

"You too, thank you," she responded, and although he wondered what exactly she was grateful of and about, he was not displeased with having decided to speak with her. Both going to a library, the two went separate but not opposite directions.

It has to be said that he enjoyed such occasions, getting beyond the greeting smile of others and although he would not fancy getting to know a stranger, knowing that there was more to someone than just their smile and casual acknowledgement of another always seemed to give him some pleasure. Hoping to have as engaging an interaction with his instructor, and perhaps even classmates, for the course he had soon to report to, he went to the library to read and print material he was sure he would need for the class.

The college library was not massive, yet it was somehow ubiquitous for near the end of Bertrand walkway one could access certain parts of the library via three sets of doors that stood guard on either side of the hall. Entering the left doors which led to the computers and printers, he made his way to the third of the quick-access computers and logged on, typing "stanboll" for username, which he greatly disliked for he almost certainly would type out the entirety of his name instead of leaving the last letters off as was necessary, and filling in the password which was always given by consecutive asterisk-like dots. Logged into his CollComm (College Community) account, he found it interesting that he never surpassed the 'five-percent used-space' mark for his allotted server or memory use, or what have you. Clicking on his "Student Space" link, he entered the more important of tools available to students for he was able to see his mail, grades, classes and other such information relevant to student life.

This was the first instance in which he enrolled in and was taking a course offered through the department of philosophy, and as such he was both curious and guarded. He felt it crucial to stay atop his responsibilities as this was new territory and so different from the sciences in which he was versed. And although he was not a poor student, finding that the instructor had sent work to be completed before the beginning of the first class, he knew that he would have to finish in forty-five minutes what could easily take an hour to complete. Wasting no more time by checking his other messages, he set to reading the paper for which he was to summarize using a syllabus-given format. Furthermore, to save even more time, he opened a Word document to begin his summary as he continued reading. The first words on the document read, "Stan Bolles, PHI 337, Thomson, A Defense of Abortion."

~~

Among the first of few students to attend class early, there was a gentleman to the rear and right with a lady to his left, two students near the front of the class to the left, and Maddie near the middle. She found herself less than comfortable. Traces of her neuroticism began to show as she began to chew her nails and the skin around them, especially her left pinky, crossed her legs, and placed her right hand between her overlapped thighs. These signs were all too undetected. The room was charged with silence, and as students began coming in one by one it diminished. Most of the students were interested in majors having a thing or two to do with medicine so the conversations were concerned with such things as vocations in medicine, future plans, and requirements which the philosophy course would meet. Most of the students were engaged in conversation with the exception of Maddie, it was not that she was uncomfortable in talking with her stranger-classmates, but she did not initiate any conversations nor seem to show interests in the others' conversations. She would have been in the way she was with situations, open to talk were she engaged, but she was not otherwise very communicative, and as such she did not join nor start any conversations. The silence returned but with no charge as the instructor, or whom the students supposed was the instructor, a tall adult woman of perhaps twenty-seven, walked in and assumed position behind the lectern and looked to the class as though she were about to address them. She was a woman of academia, what with her lunettes, hair in a bun, pallor considering the weather outside, and large but well organized tote bag. There was not even a trace of lipstick or gloss to her lips, and more, she lacked a style that would characterize a woman of her age. Perhaps, it was her T-shirt blouse and her tan trouser pants.

"Hello class, my name is Kendra Petros and I will be your instructor for this course which is Social and Ethical Values in Medicine, so if you're in the wrong class, get out," she addressed the class with the tail-end of her introduction as a joke. "I hope you were sure to read the first paper I sent you via e-mail and to your student space, we will be going over it today," her voice sounded as though it were rarely used but prepared in this occasion, for it was quiet but forceful as if the vibrations from her larynx respected the very air on which they travelled, she continued, "about A Defense of Abortion by Thomson." There was a comprehensive shuffle of papers and material as the class prepared to participate, and although there were a good number of seats empty in the back, these were with greater frequency being filled which added to the sounds in the room.

The stimuli began to fade though it remained undiminished. To Maddie the voice, and soon voices, was far away and getting even farther even though she was not daydreaming. The trouble was not concentrating or paying attention, but keeping interest in what she surely had heard once before. The instructor, for she was no professor, had probably seen Maddie before because it was not the first time she had taken the course. In fact, her first time was during the regular semester of the spring, but she had dropped the class for much the same reason she was now not paying attention nor concentrating, more or less. She was uncomfortable with the idea that she knew no one in the class and she was certain the instructor did not recognize her, and she was worried about her situation this time around as her experience initially with the course was not one she wanted repeated. She did, however, take solace in the empty seat to her left whose leading edge was aligned with her bent elbow.

Well aware of the abortion issues which she knew were going to be presented sooner than later, she noted the change when the instructor momentarily altered her routine, and stopped to take attendance. "Something," as she said, she had forgotten to do. Maddie wondered if anyone could be so excited or pleased by a course as such that they would forget to do the simpler of tasks an instructor had to do, such as taking attendance. The situation was not found to be pathetic by her, just unbecoming.

"I'll begin by calling out last names, that way any repeating first names won't be confused, and if I pronounce your last name incorrectly, correct me and I will get it right the next time." It was not long before Ms. Petros called out the name "Bolles" which seemed familiar to Maddie but she could not remember where or when she had heard the name. She searched her mind for the oddly recent memory of the name almost in synchrony with the instructor who called it out a second and third time.

∼

Stan's paper was short, about two pages, but it was well written and he knew this for he was familiar with the process of writing with little time given his experience in an English course he took during the spring semester. He hoped this would work in his favor if he left out any important or necessary information. Climbing up the stairs in Science, he was coming to the third floor which he was sure was the level on which the class would congregate for the room number was exactly the same as the level of the course which he also remembered specifically. Stan opened a door to the third floor and would have immediately searched for the 337, which was the number to the room he needed to be in and soon for he was late, had he not been presented with a split after the door. To his left he could see a hall that may have had many classrooms given the consistent interruptions of doors on the walls and the occasional garbage can outside a door or haphazardly placed in the hall. And the boards on which one could post papers and other such material told of a hall that could have students frequent it were it the regular semester. On his right was a walkway bridge that led to the other side of Science Hall and on which he was sure many of his fellow classmates must have walked for he was certain the class was on the other side. The bridge was short and with the exception of a marble floor with a light pattern like light on disturbed water, and the regular repetition of three black frames that held the windows, it was unexciting and plain.

As time is the common denominator of our lives, among other such things as oxygen and God in which we live within and die without, if it had counted the same for him as it did for Maddie when she was in the very same position in that walkway, he would have been interested to find a girl that was equally neither shy at telling the truth nor self-adjusting herself as she had done just a period before. But in its way, time has that skill of keeping knowledge from us. He chose the right way, going with his intuition, which was just as well for he began to hear a sound, the voice of a woman. He was certain. A voice of a woman who was, perhaps, in her early to mid thirties, he thought, but he was unsure as his thoughts were interrupted by what he thought to be the calling of his surname. It was difficult to miss his last name, he thought, for it was the sound, its similarity to "balls" that had gained him so much interesting, to say the least, experiences in his late childhood and even recent young adulthood. Again he heard his name being called aloud, and guessing that the instructor was taking attendance, he rushed to find the class and be marked among those present. The first classroom was to his left as he emerged out of the bridge, and happened to be the Science 337 that he was looking for. No sooner had Ms. Petros pronounced his name for what would be the final and third time did he run into the classroom as he answered, "here," with his feet slapping the ground, courtesy of his flip flops.

The class moaned a laugh as it was amused with the scene that unfolded before them in such style, Stan shook hands with the instructor who only reacted to his outstretched hand though she had no intention to shake it. As he released her wet-noodle grip, he apologized, "sorry I'm late, I was looking for the classroom and was not sure if to go left or right."

To this she responded indifferently. She was not harsh but her tone could have been considered as such, monotonously, "that's ok Mr. Bolles, just take a seat and don't be late next time." To this Stan was sure he again would hear the vocal expression of amusement from the class, but to his lack of evidence he found no one to be laughing or even smiling to the sound of his name.

He turned to look for an open seat and as though one was saved specially for him, he found one directly behind him, in front and to the left of the instructor who continued to call out names for those later in the alphabet. He noticed a young lady looking at him weirdly, with a slight squint, as he began to take his seat by first taking off his backpack and pulling out a notepad. He pretended not to notice for he was not averse to being leered at but wanted there to be some element of surprise or being caught off-guard when he would decide to look at her and display his recognition of her presence, and more, her stare.

Maddie was sure that she knew the student sitting next to her, and in fact she was sure he attended the very same high school she had attended. Why she could not remember if and when she had spoken to him was beyond her, and so she wasted little time trying to remember and hoping that he really did not recognize her. And, hopefully, would not ask if she remembered him. But she was without luck.

Stan finally turned to look at her, noticing she had stopped spying on him. The immediacy with which he recognized her would be less explained by his never forgetting faces, and was best expressed by his reaction to her, "Maddie," he exclaimed, "is that you?" As if to confirm his suspicion, and simultaneously dash Maddie's hopes of his avoidance, the instructor called out, "Welsch?" He knew her to be whom he assumed even without the aid of her surname being called aloud. The two had attended the same high school, and although they did not much interact with each other in the four years they had attended the institution, there was a preponderance of instances in which they had been around each other.

Splitting her view between the inquirers for her face was directed at the instructor, but her eyes saw Stan, she answered, "yes," a confirmation that would seem to be directed both at the instructor and Stan alike. During the taking of attendance many of the students had begun side conversations to better pass the time and, as it went, the small exchange between the two was largely inconspicuous. "Stan, right," she asked, putting little energy into gaining a confirmation she knew without doubt would come. But, again, she seemed to have the wrong expectations.

He was reminded of moments, however few, when he met members of congregation outside the normal environment which was the church as outside their element. In this case, high school. It seemed that Stan did not even bother to answer her question but continued his interrogation as though he were commissioned, "Maddie, what are you doing here? You know I didn't even know you went to school here much less that you were interested in philosophy." He began with a stern expression, by design, but then relaxed to a smile.

Her voice was near whisper when she responded, though admittedly their exchange was below the normal for speaking. "I, I'm not interested in philosophy but I have to take this class because it is one of my electives, and I go to school here Stan," she accented, responding with a smile she was not sure she wanted to share. But it was of no matter, the two had a few more exchanges that put Maddie at ease and left the two equally pleased. They were able to concentrate on the course material, which pitted the right to body against the right to life in a way that seemed unfair but just, though they both thought of the implications of knowing each other, attending the very same school, and taking the exact same course, at the same time.

At times, however, Stan's considerations were quite different from Maddie's. For instance, as the door was held open by Maddie who was with a pleasant composure as she asked, "did you drive," Stan almost did not hear her question for he was in thought about a thing the instructor had said earlier before the dismissal of class. "When arguing a point," the instructor had counseled, "it is not enough to say that something is immoral, or moral for that matter, because God said so." Stan did not like this idea but realized he did not have to, and as he was not opposed to it for it made sense, he had a few considerations with respect to the rights of humanity, and specifically, abortion. Some think that God's word is vague, indirect, or says little about abortion and whether it is a sin or not, and this he knew. But when thinking of what is said about life in the ninth chapter of the first book of the bible, he knew that to

God there was just something special in blood, or lifeblood as it were, for it was never to be consumed along with the flesh of an animal, nor shed from the vessel of man. It followed that his mental processes sought injustice in abortion by defining the act as something that shed the lifeblood of a fetus and thus deeming it immoral, but as soon as he conceived the thought it was overcome by a more cogent idea. To whom did a body belong, and was that person entitled to it, and to what extent more than another who was also entitled to it, especially given that an other's life was dependent. Are not our bodies temples unto the Almighty? But he was unsure if this applied only to believers. He was, however, very certain, for he knew by memory that 1 Corinthians 6:19, to be exact, spoke of our bodies not being our own. Furthermore, that we were to honor God with our bodies. But as it stood, there were a great many things he had still to learn, and he stored his thoughts away in the chambers, ante- or otherwise, of his mind. And that, the mind, is a wonderfully made machine for it was able to conceive, create, and amend his thoughts in an immense length of time which was impressively compressed into a total of 1.2 seconds. The amount of time it took him to sense and perceive, interpret, and formulate a response to his classmate's question.

"Yeah, I drove," he was on his third step down as he half-turned to face her as he gave his answer.

"I mean, where did you park, Main-Jefferson," she persisted. They did with small talk as they made their way down the stairs and out of the building. Onto the parking lot, Maddie pointed out her car for reasons which would have to be left to speculation. Stan described his car instead of informing her of its location. He was sure she would see him when he left, and at any rate, he wanted desperately to get home for he had skittishness about public restrooms, and so wanted to get home quickly to relieve himself.

Stan was making his second right turn after having exited Main-Jefferson, and having a penchant for instrumental jazz music, he turned on the radio which was always tuned to his favorite station other than the local-serving public news station, and looking up, he saw there was a vehicle fast behind him. He was surprised to find that a couple seconds later, Maddie's car had glided past him at a great rate which he inferred as a measure of her emotional state reflective of the situations and considerations in class which he too had experienced, but for reasons he could not possibly have surmised.

Trois

"So not only did you *not* recognize that he was at Erie with us, but you just happen to be taking the same class, at the same time?"

Maddie knew too well this would be his reaction when she told of her day's latter transpirations. "No, I mean yes, Frank," she went from ambivalence to decisiveness, "don't be sarcastic."

The timing was not the best, and she knew this, but there was not a thing she kept from Frank. She would often tell him by text messages the things that would happen to and with her, and often as it happened or soon after. But this was not something she wanted informed by a phone call or message, but, rather, in person. Frank was her very best friend, and he had the night shift at Dash's where a fair amount of the town's and city's traffic came through. Although he was used to the impromptu visits that Maddie would give, whether at his house or other locale, this visit was one of very few that she had happened on him. In fact, he could not remember the last time she would drop in unannounced at the store.

The light was loud but annoyingly inaudible. There was a buzz that was less heard and more felt, like the sensation one gets before being touched, that awareness that precedes our certainty in knowledge. The fluorescence bleached everything under it, giving the produce, freezers and their contents, and even the customers and late night shoppers a glow that was less an emanation and more an imbued reflection in that same way the sun lights the moon. As if the store was polarized, the end with the check-out lines was a hint above lively, whereas the other end, in an area which two bodies occupied, was coldly silent.

"Stop moving so much, I need to tell you this," she paced in synchrony back and forth as Frank moved containers after boxes after cases of produce and other store inventory.

"Maddie," he paused momentarily as he simultaneously projected his head and eyes with a wide look, "I'm working." Ironically, however, he stopped and listened.

"Thank you," sounding exasperated, she began, "ok, so I didn't even want to take this class because I already tried it the last semester and dropped it because I didn't do so hot *and* I didn't like some of the people in there." Frank gave two slight nods, and she continued, "well, anyways I'm sitting in class when there were a few students in there, and I'm thinking, 'ok, this isn't so bad,' you know, 'hopefully there won't be that many students in the class,' when right before it's time for class to begin a butt load of students came in and me being uncomfortable and all, they began talking as if they were friends or something. I mean, I guess I should've known that would happen, you know, nobody goes to class that early. I was early because you bailed on me, saying you had something," she paused momentarily as she tried to remember.

Frank used the iota of time to remind her, "a job interview," he semi-pouted his lips as he shaped them and his brow with disbelief.

"Right," she continued, "when you told me that, I decided to leave thirty-minutes early and make sure I got my frappuccino and found the classroom in time. Anyway, when all those people started talking and pouring in, I just hoped they wouldn't try and talk to me 'cause I wasn't in the mood, and I just wanted to see if the teacher would be the same person I had during spring." As she took a moment to prepose her last sentence, a much needed respite as both she and Frank relaxed, she caught her breath, and he cleared his mind of all that she had said. To him, he had heard nothing of importance, yet.

"That teacher was not a good fit for me," she resumed, "I never knew what was going on and, but whatever, guess who walks in just as it's about time for class to start," if she had wanted to hear Frank's guess, the terse pause was anything but indicative, "that teacher. I mean what is my luck, shit," she asked but without expecting a response. "Not only did I already sign up for her class and not take it because I didn't like her and I wasn't comfortable with everything that was going on, and all these reasons, but it's my luck that I have her after wanting to take that class and Spanish during the summer." Her voice was now characteristically femme-moderne for it was rising and often trailed with that trill in the throat which resulted in its semi-nasally sound.

She again started, "just as I was beginning to think that that class couldn't get any worse, and that I had just willingly signed up to have my already wasted summer time wasted even more, the teacher starts calling out names for attendance, which she should've done from the beginning, but that's not it," she paused to squeeze in a laugh which showed her pleasure to her thoughts in mind. With a mollified demeanor she went on, "she," referring to Ms. Petros, "called out Stan's last name and," she stopped as she saw the confusion on her friend's face, the joke was lost on him, "you don't remember what Stan's last name is do you?"

No longer facing each other, both Frank and Maddie had turned away from each other upon hearing the approach of one of the three general managers of the market. It was not difficult to hear Gary coming given his heavy footsteps and loud breathing; when Frank was first on the job, he often feared Gary was hyperventilating or asphyxiating, he was never sure, just concerned. Usually around eleven, Gary would make his way back to the "old patisserie" table on which baked goods, which had been supplanted by newer and fresher products, were placed for the penny-wise and spenders alike. But in this case store employees were attracted by the island of goodies as well. Frank knew this, but had done away with his faculties in memory for he was listening for something in particular as Maddie told her story.

Turning back, for he now realized whom had approached, Frank found Maddie feigning interests in the shelved items perpendicular to the freezer storage-box behind him. He also turned in time to catch Gary's suspicious look at both he and his friend.

"You two tight-skins better be keeping your hands off each other back here," he warned but passively, his comment was less a caution and more a joke. Frank was aware of the jocular intent in what Gary had said, but his comment was lost on Maddie who eyed the manager negatively, contrasting with Frank's smile which was accompanied by the slight shake of the head and two slow blinks. Frank liked Gary, he was his only favorite manager at the store for many reasons, but the single best reason was that Gary treated him right. When he began work at Dash's, there were a great many things he did not know that he learned from Gary. The manager seemed to always know how to teach him what he did not know, and how to gain confidence with everyone so things could run smoothly which often was what Frank wanted, no problems. He had learned that when the manager was uncomfortable with something or someone, he would invent a name or phrase which seemed to serve to attenuate his level of discomfort or the intensity of the stimulus. He seldom heard Gary use the phrase "tight skin," but he knew it to be his slang for the contemporary fashion of modern generations and a euphemism for those whose sexual orientation was men. It was unknown what Gary's term was for those whose sexual orientation was women. But this much was known, however, that Frank was gay.

"What the hell did *he* want, and what is tight-skin?" Maddie asked, exploring Frank's face as she investigated. She could tell she was not going to receive much of an answer as he stared at her, hard.

Responding with, "nothing," he raised his eyebrows signaling her to continue her story, however.

"Keeping your hands off…," she trailed, the latter being inaudible as she scowled, "any*way*, do you know what Stan's last name is?" She repeated her former question, reminding Frank where she had left off.

"Of course I know what his last name is, it was sometimes in the school newspaper for the images and cartoons he would draw," he established, but without giving Maddie what she really wanted.

She was not frustrated, just exasperated as she desperately wanted to set up to what she knew would be comedy. "Jesus Frank, just tell me his name," she paused as she set her face in expectation, head slightly turned to favor and accommodate her right ear, and the eyes raised but fixed.

"His last name is Bolles Maddie, jeez," he was both frustrated and exasperated, and his pronunciation of the name was quite different from what Maddie expected.

"Bolles," she asked in repetition, twice, as the vowel took on an "o," as in "bowls," sound. "Are you sure because," she stopped as she realized her setup to what she wanted expressed was gone and she continued with

46

the rest of the story. Less than satisfied with Frank, "never mind, you," again pausing, but momentarily for she continued, "the teacher was calling it Bolles," as she said this, with an "o" as in "jolly," instead, she looked to his face for any trace of a smile or understanding, but found none. "Bolles as in balls," she said, holding her hand in a cup directly in front of her femoral triangle as she flashed a smile that she thought would be reciprocated. "Well, whatever, I just thought it was hilarious that the teacher was calling out his name and it sounded like balls, but like you the entire class was dead silent, nobody laughed and now that I think of it I guess it was a good thing I didn't either." For a moment she seemed to have a genuine and profound contemplation which was written all over the white parchment of her face. "Then on the third call to see if he was in class, which I thought was so obvious that he wasn't, I mean after the second call you would think she knew he wasn't there. But anyway, after the third call, Stan basically jumped into the class and like tried to make friends with her, as if, and she was kind of funny 'cause even though she shook his hand, she basically blew him off and was so blasé."

She had climbed down her height of hysteria and emotion settling to a baseline in behavior which indicated something of interest in her story and could even have been observable in her slight stupor. Frank was sure she was at last going to tell of what he suspected was the underlying reason for her excitement on the entire lengthily explicated situation. Looking down as though something were serious, but lacking the edge, and far more forlorn than staid, she finished, "I was hoping he wouldn't notice me, but not only did he sit next to me, but soon after he sat down he looked at me. I know he knew because he got my name right. And as soon as we started talking even though I was hoping we wouldn't, it didn't seem so bad. And …" she left it, unfinished.

Looking as though he were expecting more, Frank gave her a sideways glance, raising his eyebrows, "and," questioningly. Frank had but one question in mind, he had come to know her in many ways and when it came to guys he knew she was not short on opinions. He wanted, simply, to know if she liked him.

Shrugging her shoulders Maddie revealed her palms while simultaneously offering her disposition, "and, you know the rest."

It was eleven o'clock. The evening shift was over and another was beginning, as such, Frank's shift was over. The two were in synchrony as they exited the market when Frank, exasperated, "I know I know the rest, what I want to know is," he was interrupted by a smiling Maddie who confidently thought she knew what he was going to say.

"You want to know if he is cute," she teethed.

Parked fairly far apart, Frank knew that they would soon have to separate and, not having his question answered, his frustration was better heard than seen. "No! Maddie, Maddie I don't care if he's cute, I know what he looks like," he stopped walking, "what I want to know is, do you like him?"

~~

Young was the day, and shining brightly but from a low angle was the sun. The rays were still quite low as they illuminated the tops of the trees and colored the sky a relaxing gray and pink, and the presence of the light served as the zeitgeber which often was the stimulus that would wake Stan from his slumber. Often, it supplanted his alarm clock. He was up right away, he often could not lay in his bed, on the floor, longer than he had to. He did not, unlike many people, dislike sleeping save when he had something very interesting, drawing perhaps, to do. He seldom would dream in his adolescence and even less so during his young adulthood; sleeping, to him, was akin to closing one's eyes and opening them shortly thereafter. But, that previous night, he had dreamt. Having gone to bed early to give himself an early start to the day, he had put to rest his thoughts on the previous night and, specifically, his encounter with Maddie. But given his dream, she competed among his thoughts that morning.

He brushed his teeth slowly because once, during his childhood, he had read that at least two minutes of brushing resulted in a thirty-percent greater clean. He was sure to get between his teeth and cheeks which, along with the tongue, he also read was important. Done, but not quite finished, he left his brush in the cup adjacent to the mirror. He never would have liked to keep his toothbrush in the bathroom where others cleaned, but having two siblings, and younger ones at that, which he shared responsibilities in training, he dealt with his skittishness. A shower followed but not before he had emptied his bowels. The entire process took fewer than fifteen minutes without his being fully dressed or properly groomed, but add this, as was his routine along with breakfast and a conversation or news, and he could ready himself in twenty minutes. This was his ritual.

No one was awake that was not out of the house already. Neither Don nor Regina, Stan's respective younger brother and sister, were yet out of their bed. Their mother had woken up before the sun and was at work that morning before it shined its rays. The house was quiet, with the exception of the birds chirping about outside, the floors cold and dry from the night, and the air seemed fresh and clean because it had not suffered the heat of day. With the blending and contrasting colors of nature just beyond the window, these were all conditions that once would have set Stan to drawing. And alone with himself, he began to be inspired in a way he had not been since his final years of high school. The new thing in life was enough to set him to drawing again. This time, however, he was creating something unusually personal, yet not about him. As he sat and prepared himself, he drew:

What began as an oval was never filled in. Radiating from the black, singular line were intricate designs; beyond description, but all before creativity. Forming a mirror, but fractional, the parchment-glass reflected part of a body. A shoulder, but no head. The beginnings of hair, part of a face before the object. Confronting the mirror, the head too was partial.

He began but did not finish the picture which he set aside to finish some other time as he had other responsibilities to attend to, and wanted to do justice to the drawing by better knowing whom it was that inspired it. In the past he would draft his images by hand, as he just had, and then transfer them to a document on a computer. Had he observed this consistency, he would have been glad to find that some things did not change. Stan opened his laptop computer, and turning it on realized he had neglected to title his unembellished and incomplete work. But this was of no matter for he wanted to wait until its completion to give it a proper title, one that would capture essence and character, concepts of matter. His cellular phone vibrated, thrice. The mobile device had been his for quite some time, and while he received a fair amount of messages, they were not infrequently ignored; it was a means to the end of transportation at one point, and a detractor from genuine communication at another. As such, he ignored it, but this is not to say he did not like to communicate with others via electronic messages. Clicking on the Internet Explorer icon, Stan entered the website address of his school and soon after navigated to his Student Space, entering into his e-mail service. He was extremely aware during his time on the computer for in regard to the internet, he knew it was an insidiously dangerous space one should not long occupy nor be occupied. There were two new messages in his inbox, and not surprisingly none of them were from Maddie.

Navigating back to his Student Space, Stan entered into his Classes section of the student page where he had a list of links into which he could enter. He chose Class Contacts. The link brought him to a page in which he had the contact information of all those involved with the PHI 337 course. That is, he was able to view the e-mail addresses of the instructors, both the graduate student and professor, and students alike. He leaned back in his chair, interlocked his fingers which arched over his head, courtesy of his arms, as he contemplated clicking on Maddie's e-mail link which would have taken him immediately to his e-mail service, allowing him to compose a message. Clicking on the link at which he had hesitated, he was brought to an almost blank page that was not in any way associated with Maddie, but had everything to do with grades. Stan had decided, after all, not to contact his new classmate for many reasons, none of which assumed that such an action was stalker-like, although admittedly, he thought it was too soon to contact her. He wanted only to inform her that in the mutual interest of both, it was best she and he transit together; to carpool. But that would have to wait.

Quatre

After almost two hours, the man lying in angle obtuse and with movements minimal was still asleep. The scene in room 257 of the second floor at Buffalo General was that of serenity. With the single television set for the two beds in as much a slumber as the patient for whom it was activated once daily, and the second bed, without a patient, occupied by a body of relation, the room was at peace with silence and in accord with love. However, there was an underlying truth that served to undermine the peacefulness of that time. The conscious body in the room was the granddaughter of the unconscious body, which had been kept at the hospital for the purpose of monitoring patient conditions.

Maddie had begun visiting her grandfather more frequently since his cerebrovascular accident which had left him unable to make use of the left side of his body. That is, he exhibited left-sided weakness at best, especially when it came to moving his foot and toes on the side, and neglect at worst as he was not only unable to use his left arm, but it seemed he almost did not care for it nor did he seem to recognize it as his. While seemingly alarming, to this Maddie and her family were not so concerned as they were to his inability to recognize them, save Grams or Happiness, Maddie's grandmother, and Maddie herself. His character underwent some changes as well, which resulted in a more or less abrasive personality that was, interestingly, context and very much person dependent. With most of Maddie's closer and concerned family members who often visited weekly, Gramps, as Maddie called him, was less agreeable and his frustration showed with almost every sentence which served to remind of his new inability to recognize his own family members, much less his care providers. Speculatively every bit as intelligent after as before the accident, Maddie feared, however, that her favorite grandparent had lost more than his freedom. Not unlike her, he was stuck and isolated.

Her attention shifted from the ceiling as she turned to face her grandfather. How ever did this being of occasional importance gain such emotional mass as to weigh so heavily on her mind, and pull with such gravity at her soul? She wondered. And she knew that his health was deteriorating as his history of smoking, which had temporarily influenced her behavior in early adulthood, further compounded his fragile condition. Heightened by her emotional state, and understandably so, her feeling of helplessness was in that she could do very little to improve his condition. She had once, or twice, considered changing her major in school from chemistry to something more or less related to healthcare, and given the recent condition of her grandfather, she had begun to consider nursing as a possible career path after her undergraduate studies. What is it she could do in the short-term that would be beneficial to him? She did not know. But on thinking what her grandfather would say, in health, when she would go to him for help, the only mental representation of his aid in need was his seldom heard admonishment, "everyone learns, sooner or later. Why not sooner than later?" Something he seldom said but had such cogence and relevance to her, particularly at that moment. She, then, decided she would change her major to nursing and pursue it with the hope of never having to feel so incapable or helpless in helping others, especially those closest to her when they were in need of help. Her resolve was slow in coming for she had long considered the idea, and an exemplar metric was the course she had enrolled in that summer as an elective which would, now given her decision, become a requirement.

It was time to leave. Her hesitation was not for any possible ostensible reasons for she knew were her grandfather aware, he would have wanted her to leave for her classes. No, her hesitation, however brief, was given by her contemplation of prayer for the ailed man before she destined for school. The idea, however inspired by her grandfather, gave her little courage to continue with the novel idea to pray for the man as she had convinced herself God would not listen to her of all people. Her perception of futility in prayer for reasons personal only added to her discouragement. She left as she came, silently, but not before touching his arm and, perhaps by way of belief, his love. Not a word was uttered between her arrival in her grandfather's room, and her departure.

~

Something, was wrong. In perhaps the second most frequented library on the campus, there stood a shocked and frustrated student at a quick-access computer near the research corner but across from the reception desk to the left of the triple doors. Clicking through the internet interface of the Student Space, Stan found in his messages that the paper which was to be read by that day was by Marquis, not Velleman. The topic for the second week of class had not changed from the topic of the previous week, but Stan had been unaware. The class was still on abortion. Having read "A Right of Self-Termination?" by Velleman, he found himself unprepared for the day's class. Knowing that he had little time as the class would convene in less than an hour, he set to reading the appropriate paper right away. In fact he did so with such immediacy that had he taken a moment to question the reasoning behind his briskness, he would find that his preparedness would not only be beneficial for class but essential in allowing him observe others, but only in reason.

It was not long after he finished the reading that Stan quickly made his way to Science Hall in which he did not take his time going up the triple set of stairs, but put a quickening in his steps. Up two flights, he sensed there was someone else about him but he was neither sure if the person was ahead of him, nor behind. As he rounded the last set of stairs to the third floor, he knew there to be someone behind him, and a classmate of his at that. He recognized the individual by her countenance which was admirable, but also by her figure which was set on a large frame making her more or less his height. And this he would not have found attractive save that her skin was quite tan, and there was something quite to his liking that he found in her gait. His attraction, however tentative, only increased as they both found mutual ground in that she had read the incorrect paper as well.

Languidly, "yeah, I read the wrong paper that is why I'm coming so late too," she said.

"I was confused on whether we were to read both papers for each week or just the one next to which my group was placed," Stan responded about the group readings in which the instructor had divided the students into two groups, a group A and a group B, which had reading assignments that alternated each week. To this effect their conversation took a negative look at their instructor, "the syllabus doesn't say much on what exactly we are to do, and in any case the fact that the both of us were confused," started Stan.

He was quickly joined by his classmate, "means that the directions were not that clear, and honestly I feel like this may be the first or second class she's taught as a grad student," she finished. Their conversation was light and in merry-making for the two were laughing with each other and making jests. Neither knew the other's name but there they were, laughing their way to class, and just on time.

Almost everyone was in class and all that were present were in seats, including the instructor. She waited for the clock to signal when she should begin that day's class, and as they all waited in the milieu of moderate conversations, there was a quiet soul who pondered but one thing. Where was Stan? Maddie was neither missing him nor desperate to talk with anyone, but he was the only person in the course with whom she had some relation. In addition, she did not want him to be late once again and create what could definitely be a scene, though it had passed uneventfully the previous time. As such, the class began to quiet as the instructor rose, and simultaneously there was audible laughter in the very hallway from which the last of the students, now seated, had come. The class was aware, as was the instructor, as was Maddie that the girlish sound was increasing in loudness indicating that the individual was coming closer. But more, there was the unmistakable timbre of Stan's voice accompanying that of the individual. His voice was not deep nor was it strong, it was neither smooth nor rough, high nor low, but a combination of all these. It was the audible equivalent of hair on skin. The two walked into class with wide smiles on their faces, Stan's with dancing eyes and his classmate's with dimples in her cheeks. Stan kept his smile as he found his seat, but his companion extinguished hers as she made her way to hers, but not before she, face downcast, defensively eared her hair. In the oblivion of time, they were neither on time nor late. Maddie did not care, however, for she was feeling almost slighted that Stan had come in laughing with this individual with whom she could currently see he was still engaged.

"You know," Stan whispered as he leaned across an open desk to his recent companion, "I never got your name." Maddie denied the feeling as jealousy but was at least aware of its presence, and she would have been happy to learn that the two were having their final exchanges.

"Amber," answered the girl.

"Stan," he added, and she nodded her head in acknowledgement.

The class discussion was on the same topic still, but from the perspective of the immorality of abortion instead of its defense. The author pointed out that conclusions on the subject matter were either "generated by seriously confused philosophical arguments," or "irrational religious dogma," to relay the purpose of the essay which was to "undermine this general belief." Class arguments on principles, which were at times broad and too often embraced much, or were narrow and left much out, were made to aid in describing the boundaries by which humanity exists. To aid in defining personhood. This was necessary as a beginning point for which death, whether that of a developed human or fetus, would then be considered for its morality or immorality. With the discontinuation account considering the value of a future and the related "future like ours" concept discussed, along with the desire account which argued that one need show interests or care for life so it may not be taken away, the class was nearing its end when Stan began thinking. Yes, Marquis was arguing against abortion, but the definition of life was not clear. When did it begin and at what point was it fully realized? With respect to an abortion itself, was not there a string of other immoralities that went without questioning of their moral status? These unquestioned resulted as an ultimate moral issue, death and life, on which Stan had many questions but very few answers. He hated his ignorance in the Word, and he also loathed the little he knew for it never was quite enough.

He knew that Job, both the book and the man, provided a profound statement of God's justice in light of human suffering, especially the suffering of the innocent. Stan was sure that God was acknowledged as the ultimate authority on lives and life when Job said, "*I will say to God: Do not condemn me but tell me what charges you have against me,*" and, "*your hands shaped me and made me. Will you now turn and destroy me? Remember that you molded me like clay. Will you now turn me to dust again?*" (*Job 10:2,* & *Job 10:8*, respectively) Was this not to be the same authority to which we turned in issues minor or major, trivial and ultimate? He did not like that the Word was discounted in argument against abortion, perhaps because he could not help but place himself in the center of main focus as ever once being a baby or fetus. He was convinced that to live was to have choice, to choose red or blue, left or right, life or death. As babies are and will always be, as he was, lacking the power of choice or its expression for as the instructor had mentioned multiple times, "the lack of evidence is not evidence of a lack," to take away life at that beginning was to preclude all their choices, good or bad, poor and sound. The love of God, of a father, of a mother is what it takes to give a baby a chance at life. A chance at choices which, once they begin making them, are overwhelmingly reciprocated in that beautiful love a child has for a mother. It was not in the place of man to decide on such matters; *Did not he who made me in the womb make them? Did not the same one form us both within our mothers?* (*Job 31:15*) But, again, he was unsure if this applied only to believers. That day's paper was by Don Marquis, which Maddie coldly reminded him when he asked. Maddie was something less than pleased, and Stan was not completely unaware.

With less than two minutes left in class time, students were becoming antsy and anticipatory. Maddie especially could not wait to leave as she frequently stole looks at the clock on the left wall. "What," Stan asked, he realized later than sooner that she was frequently leering at him.

Defensively and with a measure of umbrage, "nothing," replied Maddie. There seemed to be a long pause in the last thirty seconds of class when Maddie continued, leaning over, "I thought you were gonna be late again… today." The class was dismissed and students were shuffling out the door very much in the same way they did during the last class, with the exception of a few slinking back to talk with the instructor, and Maddie, who patiently waited for Stan as he collected himself and prepared to make his exit from the classroom. "I know why you asked me that, you know, because you thought I was looking at you," Maddie began, "and I was, not because I thought you were gonna be late again, but, well I did think you were gonna be late, but because I was just surprised when you came in laughing with that girl, which," she smiled irresolutely, "you don't even know."

Stan was busied placing his belongings and contents into his backpack and seemed not to give her his full attention, but given her joke, he was prompted to pause, however briefly, to give her a moment of his faculties in attention. "So, you were giving me looks because you were wondering why I came to class laughing, with a girl, that I don't know," he asked in a start-stop sort of manner.

They both started making their way to the door when they were interrupted by a monotonous instructor who admonished, "Mr. Bolles, try not to be on time next class, because when you're on time you're late, and if you're late again you will lose a grade point in this class," she must have paused for effect, "every time." They both stopped, looked at the instructor in unison, but neither said a thing, save that tacit expression that was hidden in mutual smiles.

Walking out first, "she's just a classmate Maddie, you know," Stan was nearing the door, and opened it when he reached it, holding it for Maddie. They walked down the first flight of stairs together, but in silence.

"I know," came Maddie's terse but long-in-coming response, "I just," she paused, "anyway, I wanted to tell you something, well suggest something, anyway."

"Ok, I want to tell you something too, but go ahead," Stan admitted and urged simultaneously.

"Oh, really," she seemed genuinely delighted, "what is it, you go first," she commanded as her simple request was accentuated by an abrupt arrest.

"Nothing really, you know, just that you surprised me with your honesty when you told me why you were peeking at me," he smiled to take off whatever hard edges were in his words for he could see her smart in face.

Maddie now held a blank stare, blank and stark, she asked, "is that, that's it? That's what you had to tell me?"

Stan was confused, he thought that what he told her caused her some discomfort or abashment but it seemed she had wanted to hear something that was more piquant. As they were almost to their respective cars, this time they had parked closer but not quite next to each other, Stan did away with these thoughts as he inquired into what she had wanted to share with him earlier, "so what did *you* want to tell me?"

"Ok, while I know that we don't have school next week, or I mean next Tuesday, because Ms. Petros is giving us off for that conference," she said, shaking her head as if to clear the imaginary cobwebs that crossed about her mind just moments before, "I was thinking we could commute together. You know, ride together, carpool," she added, again tossing her head, but just to the side as if to weigh the newly expressed thoughts against his unshared response.

He smiled, dropping, "yes, that's a good idea." He had a few things in his arsenal of pretenses, "but how will either of us know when and where to get each other because I don't have your number or your e-mail." He feigned ignorance at knowing her contact information, but not before he pretended to almost forget posing the question. In an almost similar fashion, with respect to the pretenses, she responded suavely, "I'll e-mail you," she responded as she opened her car and entered it in fluid motion. They were both weary and had a relatively short but all too long drive. But that night they were pleased and all smiles.

Cinq

Honk-Honnnk! Maddie was sitting in her car outside a
mid twentieth-century home with four symmetrical
columns that held a classic porch enveloping three beige
chairs, a long low table, and a brown lattice-like bench.
There was a set of stairs that led up to the porch which
spanned the entire front of the house and had a set of
windows, one on each side of the centered door. The
lack of a garage added to the symmetry of the house, but
the unilateral driveway to the right that led to a trellis-
like structure, up which a prominent vine and assorted
plants grew, did away with this symmetry along with the
tree and above-ground pool on the opposite and rear side
of the house. Honk! She again activated her car horn. A
few moments later, however, she received a call from
Stan who informed her he was not quite ready to leave;
he was working on his paper still. The two had
exchanged numbers via e-mail on the Tuesday they
received off from school, but not having named the
contact as Stan, Maddie was a little apprehensive at
taking the call she received. "Hello," she was confident
as she was almost certain whom had called, "ok, well
I'm coming in then," she informed Stan as she ceased
the engine while opening her car door simultaneously.

As she approached the front steps the front door to the
house opened, and occupying its entrance was Stan who

then, upon seeing her, quickly ran deep into the house. "You can come in," he yelled, "I'm still working on my paper," he conditioned. She walked in, and laying before her but to the left of the door was a set of stairs leading up to the second floor. With its white-pink composition and texture, it resembled a sharply corrugated tongue within a very cavernous mouth. The runway-hallway on which Stan had took off was to the right of the stairs and directly in front of Maddie. It led to a kitchen counter that doubled, increasingly as she walked farther into the chambers of the house, as a breakfast table. She was not quite looking for Stan, but when he informed, "I'm in here," she was quickly aware of his location as she turned left and found him sitting at a doubled desk; a desk with another structure atop which allowed for storage of things such as office material but was stuffed with books and papers. Stan was busy typing away on his laptop-computer at the desk which was opposite a mahogany-colored love-seat perpendicular to a full-sized couch of the same color but of different design. All the furniture, including the desk, were on one side of the spacious room, the side on which Maddie stood. On the other were the entertainment electronics such as the television, a radio, and what looked to be a video game. The room was not adorned, but was spacious enough to be best for children and young adults alike.

Maddie did not sit long when Stan finished the paper and indicated he was ready to go, and although she was not quite ready to leave herself, her reluctance did not show as she greeted Regina, Stan's sister with whom she had been engaged, goodbye. The two made their way out of the house with Stan giving elder sibling-like instructions which had more or less to do with how his two younger siblings were to conduct themselves in his absence. "I like her," Maddie mentioned, referring to Regina, as Stan sealed the cabin of the car by closing the passenger door.

"Yeah, you like her because you don't really know her," he responded, "she's a little manipulator, and an adroit one at that," he joked. The remainder of their conversation was exchanges in niceties wrapped in complementary phrases such as "nice… family," and "… thank you for waiting," but it was a short time before they began something of more substance.

Observing her driving behavior, Stan was compelled to ask, "should you be driving so fast, I mean you've been hitting all the lights and I'm concerned that not only might you get a ticket, but you're wasting a lot of gas too." Maddie was zipping in and out of spaces while outmaneuvering her slower commuters. Unfortunately, her efforts were wasted at times as she would either misjudge lights or find herself slowed by cars ahead of her, and in both lanes. She was, however, adhering to the unwritten 'nine you're fine, ten you're mine' rule of driving. That is, supposedly, nine miles per hour above the speed limit a driver is without the notice of law enforcement, but ten miles per hour or more over and the driver speeds at the risk of a ticket.

"I wanna get there in time to study a little for the test," she replied, "besides, this is how I drive and," looking over to Stan, she added, "don't worry, I'm good at it. And besides my boyfriend says that gas is way cheaper here than in Buffalo, so it's not a big deal even though you're right that gas is mad expensive."

"You have a boyfriend," Stan asked, less taken by surprise and more by wonder. "What's his name?"

"Hhgrgh," she let out a deep sigh to which Stan smiled quizzically with a furrowed brow. "Yeah I have a boyfriend but I don't even want to think about him right now," she concluded. But after only a few moments of silence, she restarted, "his name is Drake, and he lives in Cheektowaga or Buffalo or wherever. I don't even care," she muttered under her breath. Stan's silence goaded her on, "yeah," she sighed, with eyebrows arched and forehead wrinkled, she added, "he's a real catch."

"Drake of Buffalo, who actually lives in Cheektowaga, but *is* a catch," Stan made a jest that she took as further encouragement.

"Well, his last name is Wittram, but who cares, it's not like I'll take it, we're never getting married, you know, the stupid idiot won't even have sex with me."

The short silence was almost too long when Stan saved, returning Maddie's peer with a gaze, by saying without emotion, "that's unfortunate… but I hate to worsen whatever your situation is by saying you should have a lot more in common with another and a lot more to do with someone else before you consider having sex with them."

She looked to him, and finding his sincerity, responded, "oh I know. We knew each other for a little bit before we started dating and we did do a lot together, but ever since school started, he seems cold and doesn't want to do anything. He's distant and I'm pretty sure he's cheating or something, but the hard part is that *I'm* trying not to," she accented, bunching her fingers to a point directed at her sternoclavicular notch. She was fairly animated now. The minority of her movements were through the instruments that were her left arm and right foot, while the majority of movements were through the remainder of her body which was engaged in the physical manifestation of her thoughts. Stan was attentive, the edge of entertainment held back by concern, however superficial. She continued, "I'm serious, the way I'm looked at, and the way guys are with me I could easily cheat, but I don't." They stopped at the last red light before a small stretch onto the campus, and acutely angling her elbow on the door, near the window, Maddie rested her head in her palm. She then looked at Stan, hard, saying, "you're probably the only guy I know that doesn't want to have sex with me." There was silence before she added, "other than Drake, of course."

"I suppose I'm glad you think that, but you're right. I believe you shouldn't have sex until you are married," Stan returned, holding a small smile, for he knew there was a subconscious, an animal within that may very well have wanted what he only just denied in mind. For it had used his very conscious and so-aware eyes to carefully delineate her outline that day.

Searching for Main-Jefferson and concentrating on the road signs and lanes on the campus, Maddie's attention was divided between this task and her response. She threw back a thoughtless scoff, "what are you a Christian?" She was now parking.

Stan lightened what he thought was quickly becoming a dark mood as he breathed out a smile, "yeah, if you consider it praying and worshipping God while reading the bible and following the Word, then yeah, I'm a Christian."

When Stan made to open the door, not having continued nor chuckled to imply jocularity in his comment, Maddie looked at him, searching his face to discern something. "Are you serious," she asked.

As he caught her gaze and barely formed, "what? Yeah, I'm serious," he answered, posing his own question, "why, don't I look it?"

She was awkward, especially given her comment, "it's a good thing we are riding together 'cause I'm gonna probe you as if *I'm* an alien." She bade him goodbye as she left to print her study material, visit Ms. Petros, and prepare for the test, though not in that particular order. And Stan went straight to Science 337, he too was going to study, but in the company of others.

~

Beginning the third class with which they would share with each other, the Social and Ethical Values in

Medicine class was more comfortable and relaxed which could be seen in casual conversation, but more so in the content which expressed little, if any, worry on the imminent assessment. The hours during which the class assembled always took from the evening to night, and so the temperature was cooler than during the day, but not cold. Accordingly to individual differences and or preferences, students dressed variedly from scant cladding to full clothing; one student, in particular, donned sweatpants and a hoodie sweatshirt. Stan wore a gray T-shirt and his dry-fit pants which, though they were the same length as his legs, exposed his ankles when he sat. Maddie smoothed blue shorts under her form-fitting T-shirt which was very pink. It was not that she was warmer than Stan, but the difference between the lower-temperature ambient air compared to her body temperature was lesser than that difference in Stan, and this is how he came to understand her choices, both in fashion and the use of the A/C when driving. It was time to take the test and everyone was quiet, seated. This time, Maddie sat to Stan's left. The test was administered at the beginning of class, and upon everyone finishing, Ms. Petros began to lecture. The topic was euthanasia, or was it assisted suicides? Maddie did not care. She was pondering Stan's words and position during the last of their major exchanges.

~

"So," she paused, "you're saying that you wouldn't have sex with someone, even if you loved them a lot, until you were married to them," Maddie asked. The two had been on the road for more than fifteen minutes when Maddie finally broached the subject in a manner to her liking. Before Stan could answer, she continued, "what you're basically saying is that if a girl, a hot girl was willing to have sex with you, and she showed it, you know, most times you don't have to say it, that you wouldn't do it with her?"

This time she waited, and he responded. "Yes, I am saying just that, but a little more. I would not have sex until I was married because of the love I have for God, and through God, for that person."

She held a quizzical look, "what, that doesn't even make sense." She made a right turn into the first of Tim Horton's as one headed into town. As she found a parking spot, Stan pondered how to better inform her of his beliefs. The nature of their interaction had suddenly become more complex, sensitive, and tense, but he thought the philosophy course may have lent him some skills necessary in the moment and believed by God's grace the situation was within his abilities. Maddie geared the car to park, turned to Stan with both her arms on the wheel, and asked, "hypothetically speaking, if I showed I wanted to have sex, like right now, right here, and you saw that, you wouldn't go for it?" There was a slight discomfort in her sound, but whether it was due to shame, guilt, or to save face and respect his, is a mystery.

His reply was terse, "No." If his reply were her decisive cue, she did not hesitate as she opened her door, and this signaled they were both to exit the car.

"I know you already told me we were stopping here, but why are we here again?" Stan may have felt it was his turn to be inquisitive and lighten the mood, or he was genuinely ignorant of Maddie's particular desire for a sweet or caffeinated beverage.

"I just want to grab a few things, a drink and something to eat."

There were customers in the café, which was not surprising to Stan though the hour was late. What he found interesting, however, was the age of the people sitting at two separate tables. Three women and two men who were easily over fifty years of age were seated, two of the three women with one gentleman at one table and, presumably, an old couple at another. Catching his view, Maddie informed Stan that the old couple reminded her of her grandparents, and to this she gave a wry smile and sighed. Stan imagined that her expression meant something but before he could think on it, Maddie further explored question-land. This one was rhetorical, "so you're a Christian, you know I may have known that about you." She walked and talked without looking at him, but interspersed between her inquiries and comments she would throw out, "do you want something," or, "you have to try this," and Stan followed her both by conversing and by walking. "You know, I just can't believe you are a Christian, I mean it's like

I've known you for so long, but not really known you," she paused, and it seemed she was about to happen on a realization of her subconscious which had composed a liking of her companion that was a little less than correct, but she did not, asking, "you know?" Stan shrugged, having nothing more to say, it was almost clear that he wanted to go home or be someplace else. She sighed ambivalently, sipped on her beverage as she paid for it and the other bagged goods she chose. The two walked back to the car in silence, Stan ahead of Maddie.

Stan's house was about twenty minutes away when they left the lot, but Maddie's car was five or less turns from its destination thirteen minutes later. "So, from the sound of it," this time Maddie began to speculate, "you go to church, you…," she was cut off by Stan who responded with a fake chuckle.

"Yeah, I go to church."

"You go to church, you're always a good person," to this Stan looked at her interestingly, as opposed to impassively nodding his head along with what she said. She smiled dryly and continued, "you read the bible," and pausing, she then added as a jest, "and I bet you've never had sex."

Taking her silence as the termination of her spiel, Stan responded, "Yeah, I mean no, I've never had sex, and I guess I do all those things you listed, though it's not easy to always do what's good."

They were almost to his house when Maddie said, "it's just that I can't believe this, but I believe you, you know," she asked, looking to him. To this there was no response. Making the right onto Stan's street, Maddie chuckled and aired, "yeah, that's all good but I bet you've never even kissed a girl."

Stan was not happy with her remark. He dragged, "and I actually have, so you should probably stop assuming things you don't know."

To this she was sensitive as she parked in his driveway. Remorse, and almost in monotone, she apologized, "sorry," she paused. "I, it's just that I used to consider myself a Christian too, and, of course I'm not now," she joked. "I mean I believe in God, I just don't like how some people are, even my grandparents, you know" she again paused, adding, "and I've had sex, before being married, and like it, you know."

Maddie was not at all shy at telling Stan some of her concerns for her grandfather. At this point her lack of inhibition was complete. Had not she felt guilt at offending Stan, she would have given more details and discussed at length her grandfather's condition. As such, she only shared, "the other week, I didn't pray for my Gramps because I didn't even think *I* was worth it, you know? He hasn't been getting better and I think if anyone can help him, only God can. And I hope God doesn't look at me to make him better, but looks at his heart 'cause he's a great grampa." There was quiescence, but it seemed necessary.

As if the two were observing a moment of silence or together in prayer, Maddie and Stan were wrapped in taciturnity with their faces downcast and barely lit by the ambient reflective light. Finalizing what Maddie began in apologizing, Stan comforted her, "you're alright Maddie. The truth is that some Christians are like you. In fact I would say you and I are the same in God's eyes. We both are sinners, and with no one being sinless, the only difference is that God forgives you *when* you ask for forgiveness." Reassuring her, he continued. "Even in my abstinence, I honestly would love to believe it's my love for God that I follow the Word, and I honestly hope it is. But I know I want my virginity to be something I can proudly give the one I love, because I can't promise her what I can't control, and even then I sometimes pray I am able to hold to my resolve. For your grandpa, whatever his condition, pray. Even if you don't think God will hear or answer because, bottomline, it's not about you. Right? It's about your grandpa." To this there was a momentary cessation of speech.

Maddie looked as if she was going to smile, but did not, and breaking the silence, admitted, "but, I mean I know that God can forgive me and make my sins like they never happened, but sometimes I don't even feel worthy, you know. Like, I don't want to pray for forgiveness and not mean it. Like sex is good for me, and I really like it, and I don't think I can give it up for God, even though I know it's a sin. And what's worse is that I believe in God and know there are only two sides, only good and bad, that there is no middle. So it's like I want to be good, but this one thing makes me bad, you know, and it makes me mad sometimes. And at other times," hushed, "like now, it makes me really sad at the same time."

Stan was preparing to leave the car, but sensing that Maddie wanted something of a response to her statement, he further soothed her. "Well, don't beat yourself up, too much that is. That sounds really sincere and legitimate, but remember that God is the one you need to talk with. After all, that's what prayer is for, right. I really think that when you decide what is most important, then it will be easier to remedy your situation, especially if you pray on it. And it's not like the sex is the bad thing, right, God made that for us. It's the timing, like in most things. I'm sure you would agree with me when I say that it is not bad to have a child or children, but when you're not ready to take care of the child or those children, then that's where it's bad. Think of our class arguments: A person has the right to have a child, or children, is the first premise. To have a child, one must be able to successfully care for it is the second. I know it's probably not the best argument, but the conclusion would be that anyone can have a child as long as they can take good care of it. Anyway, I have to go, I'm tired and I'm sure my mom is wondering what's taking me so long, especially considering we're here. Talk to you next week."

Maddie pleasantly cocked her head, "how about tomorrow," she asked. As Stan mulled over her suggestion, she added in question, "e-mail or text?"

"You let me know," Stan answered.

"Ok. Bye," replied Maddie as Stan closed the door. Differently, she looked at him differently. And he, her.

Six

Fft-fft, two shots flew by, and off in the distance one could hear the sounds of quickly decompressing gasses shortly followed by the hard splashes characteristic of exploded paintballs. "Stay low," the first player signaled to the second in hopes they would not be discovered by the opposing team. But the second player, perhaps under the impress of bravado or genuinely invested in the success of the Two, or two-man team, jumped over the short wall that served as their protection against the barrage of paintballs, mouthing, "I'll draw their fire." As if an attractor of the balls of colored liquid, the second player was riddled with smears, streaks and splashes of paint, but this allowed the first player the opportunity to tag the surprisingly few players that numbered three. The situation unfolded as though it were practiced or rehearsed.

"Nice shots," complemented the second player as he undressed his colorful vest and upper protective garments in transit with his teammate.

"That was a foolish move," the first player threw back. He too was taking gear off his person and placing them on the multilevel counter that was specific for items and gear. To the receptionist-clerk-cashier-like Soft-staff, "let the owner know that we enjoyed the trial."

"Yeah, but we got the job done. I mean, there's no way we were going to take those guys head on. They're good," the second player said, the only of the two still doffing his equipment as the other player began to take a leave.

"Will that be all," asked the Soft-staff. Given a head nod by Stan, she inquired but with complement, "that was a good Two, you guys have any suggestions or thoughts?

Holding a finger to the lady, Brent, Stan's acquaintance for some time, responded, "yeah, but I have her e-mail," referring to the owner. "But hang on," turning to Stan, "hey man, are you sure you want to call it quits, I mean we only had three plays. Maybe we should try a game, one where we're not on sides."

The venue was recreational, and the location was prime. Situated within 30 miles of most post-secondary academic institutions in Western New York, SoftSpot was one of the newer businesses to open in the area, and with potential, and catered to broad and specific groups of people simultaneously. The dark, metallic sheen of the outside sign hinted little at what went on in the building, and the business name yielded more but still incomplete information about the 2495, Main street venue. The red-brick building had undergone some changes to become an establishment for indoor airsoft and paintball recreational activities. However, to the frustration of SoftSpot's beginning and growing customers and players, the business did not yet have appropriate equipment for airsoft plays, especially with respect to tagging.

"That'd be interesting Brent, but I don't want it to seem like we're taking advantage of this free trial by the owner." Stan was interested in another Play, or Game, as Brent had suggested, but having spent nearly two and a half hours "playing," Stan felt he needed to invest his time in other matters.

"Dude, she wants us to play so we can give her feedback to make the place better. I mean, we're the ones who are technically doing her a favor," responded Brent.

The Soft-staff, having watched the exchange between the two, prepared to give new gear to Brent, and relinquish all the gear that Stan had returned. What she looked for, which came shortly, was his agreement. "Alright, let's do this and be done with it," Stan responded, concealing as best he could his excitement at the prospect of having another Play without having to part with any unit of money.

"Alright," exclaimed Brent as Stan finished the accord. "Besides I want to beat you at something I have a chance in since you seem to be doing very well in the lady department," added Brent.

To this Stan took notice and continued donning his equipment, but slowly. "What are you talking about, the lady department?" Brent smiled, but before he could give his response, the Soft-staff informed, "your Game will begin in 30 seconds ladies." Brent turned and smiled at her, but Stan ignored the two completely as he made his way to a strategic area from which to begin the game.

The play field was not unlike a maze, a labyrinth of sorts. With furniture in certain areas, appliances in others, and even a bathroom that was complete, the field was that of a home, with the exception of a roof for which the vaulted ceiling of the factory-like building served as one, however unnecessary. The walls allowed players and objectives alike a hiding place, protection, and proved to be of strategic importance. There were two other players in the field, and the objective of the game was to find one of several weapons caches from which more ammunition could be acquired, for this was often necessary to win the game.

Each player begins with four paintballs, the amount of players in the field. While it seems only three paintballs need be expended by any player to Tag the other three players, this is not the case, however. With a Tag comes extra Charges, or lives, and as such any player can become very difficult to Discharge with Tags. A Charge is given for every Tag, and should a Tag be the final Discharge of a player, then the total amount of Charges that player had is awarded to the tagging player, provided the pre-reward Charges of the tagging player are not greater than or equal to the awardable Charges during the Discharging Tag. That is, all things being equal with every player introduced into the field holding one Charge, any player Discharging an other receives two Charges. One for a Tag, and the other as the total amount the discharged player held. As complexity in the logistics of the plays and games increases, the more the Field, or Soft-staff, is involved to assure fairness and appropriate playing activity. As such, while player honesty, which is often helped along by indicative, colorful Tags, is usually relied upon during Play, greater involvement by Soft-staff is necessary in the Games and greatly reduces player responsibilities during plays.

"Don't tell me you don't know what I'm talking about," began Brent before the triple ring of the commencement tone, "I've seen you with a girl a couple times." In between intense play and attempts at other players, Brent's vocal output rose and fell with his physical efforts.

With walls without ceilings, Stan took up position on top of a fridge and behind a wall. From this position, he was sensitive to all the movements on the ground, and as such was keen to Tag one of the players who attempted to furtively Tag another. Not having Tagged another player, that player was Discharged, and so eliminated. This was just as well to Stan for in Tagging the player, he gained knowledge of another player hidden somewhere in what represented a living room. However, Stan was uncertain whether the player was Brent or just the third player.

The game had picked up in intensity and, given the distance between Brent's location and Stan's, Brent was now shouting to converse. "She's pretty hot man, I've seen her pictures on Facebook and some of her comments show that you two have been doing more than hanging out." Brent had, more or less, given away his position by speaking to Stan, but one could speculate that he did so to draw him out and to chance catching the other players in crossfire. The third player, within earshot of Brent, started to make her way toward him. Unable to see this, but with some intuition to movement and location, Stan repositioned. Behind a love seat from which he could view the rear of the kitchen, from which he came, he had crossed the dining room in which there was no trace of paint from his Discharge of the eliminated player. In addition, he could partially see the halls connecting the kitchen rear to the living room, which he occupied. He did not have the angle for the shot, but, given Brent's potential location, he knew she would cross the hall sooner than later. A moment after the thought, the third player scurried from a door to the bathroom in a roundabout way, along the wall, toward the far end of the field where Stan, and he imagined she too, suspected Brent might be. Stan had the shot, but when he took it, he missed.

The player must know where he was, he suspected, and having both his location and Brent's, relatively, he knew she had the upper hand in the Game, especially as he did not know where the weapons cache was located, nor if it was acquired. Stan did not risk holding his position for he knew his shot betrayed it, and knowing he had but two paintballs remaining, he could not afford to miss on his next attempt. With the marker nozzle trained on the position Stan last viewed the third player, he yelled, "what do you mean more than hanging out?" Ostensibly, this action was to betray his position but preserve his person, as he quickly crawled from behind his protection, while simultaneously eliciting a distracting response from Brent.

There was no response, neither from Brent nor the third player as Stan investigated the position he knew she last occupied. As such he proceeded cautiously by what may have been the garage or basement door as he made way into what could serve as a den, fireplace included. It seemed the third player had resolved to pursue Brent for what it was worth, for Stan found her crouched by a once magnificent, but dilapidated, entertainment station, peering through the hollows and holes. He was silent, stealthy and catlike. With his entirely black gear, mask, vest and trousers, he was not unlike a contemporary ninja. Within meters of her position, he could see her backside and right shoulder on which he took the shot. Tagged, there was a feminine, "damn it," from the girl as she looked back while standing up. As she walked by him, with a scowl on her face, to exit the Field, there was an almost-immediate response by Brent.

"It's just you and me now buddy." The sound came directly from behind the kitchen windows, informing of Brent's location as on the sun-deck-like platform on the opposite side of the sliding doors through which the second-eliminated player had peered.

Agonizing over how possibly he was going to open the sliding door without notice or incident, Stan rested against the wall as he formulated a plan to Discharge Brent and secure a victory. An acute angle formed between the wall and his legs, and his arms rested against his torso and were occupied by his marker. Stan's head, caressed by his mask, rested against the wall as well though he frequently scanned his surroundings to ensure the maintained secrecy of his position. At this point the Game was very intense for Stan, and excited, he knew he needed some focus. Brent most likely had found the weapons cache and acquired more ammunition for himself while he, Stan, had Discharged the other two players, Stan conjectured. This, however, was speculation. It was of no consequence should he be incorrect for he knew that having acquired three extra Charges, he was going to have to be Discharged four times before being eliminated. Although Brent, again, most likely retained his four paintballs, had he not misfired or missed any shots. Then the very least Stan had to do, he assured himself, was Tag Brent before he could Tag him.

Should Brent be able to Tag him before he could preempt the shot, he would indeed lose the Game for Brent would, assuming he found the weapons cache, have acquired more paintballs in addition to the four necessary to completely Discharge Stan and already in his possession. With something that resembled trepidation, though very minute, he forcefully, and so quickly, pushed open the sliding door and approximating Brent's location, exposed only his marker and squeezed out his final paintball. There was nothing. No indication of victory as given by Brent's acceptance of defeat. No report of the paintball as it burst. Most importantly, no single tone to signal the simultaneous end of the Game by final Discharge.

Stan peeked out on the dark-gray sun deck. There were two beach chairs and a plastic chair, a patio table with an umbrella piece instead of the appropriate parasol, and railings wide enough to sit on comfortably. There was, however, no Brent. It seemed his remaining opponent had given him the very same medicine he only recently tried to administer. Also lacking was evidence of the paintball Stan released as the soft foam material on the outer walls of the field, which served as the background to the all too empty scene, may have absorbed the impact of the projectile, preventing it splash. Quick to return his attention, Stan expected to see movement or even find his acquaintance in the room. However, he found his expectations, a fear, allayed. He closed the door and locked it, precluding the possibility of a surprise from that outside. He began to make his way toward the direction from which he came, but found himself pondering why some of the drawers and doors on the damaged entertainment station were opened.

Having searched through most of the compartments on the tarnished furniture, Stan found nothing until he examined the upper left compartment that held a picture of, not ironically, a group of people similarly clad in red and black uniform, gathered together on a field some sunny day, presumably for the picture, and all brandishing a paintball marker of one design or another. Behind the picture was a solid green box that seemed neither touched nor open. Cautiously scanning behind to check for the long-disappeared Brent, he knelt with the box as he attempted to determine how to open it. Strongly right-handed, he placed his marker between his right thigh and the crook of his right elbow as he reached to manipulate the box held firmly against the floor by the tight grip of his left hand.

He was quiet and quick, measured and methodical. Within seconds he had the box opened and found the container that held the paintballs. It was too late. In retrospect, he knew the box was much too light to have held as many paintballs as the rounded square-container suggested. He had wasted valuable time on a task that yielded absolutely nothing. He was surprised at his findings, but matters went from bad to worse when he had the hair-raising sensation of a presence behind him. The presence was all too familiar, and that of Brent's. Stan had no recourse. He was dry, and though the thought of removing the marker in Brent's possession fired in his mind, he knew scrimmaging was not permitted in plays. There were, he was told, other weapons caches with variable content, but the predicament seemed feckless.

He was still Charged, Brent had not Tagged him. Stan searched his mind for anything to continue the delay of the inevitable. As his back was to his acquaintance, he rose slowly with his hands up, shoulder height and apart. "What did you mean by 'more than just friends'," he asked.

"You tell me," Brent's response was taunting.

"Brent, I don't know what the heck you're talking aba…," fft, fft-fft-fft. Brent Tagged Stan from about three meters away, an attempt on Brent's part to attenuate the force of impact. The single tone rang, it was the end of the Game. "Dude, that hurt," Stan scowled, reaching for the nape of his lower back as he spun to face Brent, "and why didn't you shoot when you first had me?"

"Why don't you tell me what's going on with you and that girl," Brent retorted.

Stan was not at all pleased with the outcome of the Game, or the close shot Brent took at his back. In addition, Brent's incessant inquisition only served to further compound Stan's ire, resulting in, "her name is Maddie, not that girl. Back off Brent, I don't know why you continue to ask about her when you don't know who she is," stopping for emphasis, "and she obviously doesn't know who you are. Besides it's none of your business."

"It is my business, goddamn it Stan," Brent was getting frustrated, but for reasons that can only be speculative. "I dormed with you for nine months, nine months dude. I know you," he began, but as they had made their way back to the service counter, Brent was interrupted as they were served by the very same Soft-staff as previously.

"Who won," the lady asked. The question must have been rhetorical for she very well could have been one of the staff involved in the mediation of play during the Game.

"Shut up," was the sharp response from Brent. Turning back to Stan, "I know that you don't like any or most of the girls we've been around in the past nine months. Not even the ones that were interested. I know that you don't pay attention to them for one reason or another, even when they live on the very same floor as we do," Brent was now gesticulating and very engaged in his revelation, "even, and especially when they're next door."

As riled as Brent seemed, Stan was just as irate, but he knew to cool and collect himself. Calmly, "you don't know jack about me Brent," Stan shrugged off, seemingly, both his gear and Brent's comments.

"Yeah," interrogatively, "alright," he responded unconvincingly. Having made his way to the car with Stan in tow, he stopped before opening the door, turning back to him. "You know, I don't give a damn if you like her. I really don't care if you don't either. I just maybe wanted to know whom you were spending time with when I'm gone, and even that you might like them so we may talk about *you* for once." Composed and dispassionate, but unfinished, he continued, "and maybe I don't know you that well, but you can't blame me for trying, after all that's what a friend does."

Stoic, Stan encouraged, "I've never seen you so honest, please continue."

"Sometimes I don't know that you realize or even think that we're friends," was Brent's conclusion after a reluctant nod.

Trying to find meaning in his words, "I," but finding none, his demeanor was guilt. "Yeah, I apologize, and you're right to be in my business, even though you come across boorish." His expression comprised the minimum of a smile.

Brent's facial response was not in kind as he was not convinced, "Uh-huh," he nodded insincerely. "Oh, come on. I don't mean to get emotional, but you're the one who tells me that it's not a real apology unless the person says 'I'm sorry'."

Teething a smile, Stan relented, "alright, Brent. I'm sorry," pausing for effect and sincerity, "I'll tell you all that you want or need to know, but first I think you should apologize to the lady who served us."

~

"Oh, and be sure to let me know how the App you're working on is going," Stan remembered to remind Brent. Having arrived home on a more profound note than that with which he left, Stan was pleased to find that he could restore a remiss friendship on his part, one he may have taken for granted.

With a heavy sigh, "well, it's going, but you'll be the first to test it," Brent informed, inserting the car into drive as he prepared to depart.

Grateful, "alright, and thanks. Take the thruway to get home, it's faster." Stan replied, to which Brent gave his signature goodbye as he drove away and pointed a non-incriminating index finger to Stan simultaneously.

With the front door locked, Stan opted to take the side door that led directly into the heart of the house, the kitchen. If the car of Japanese make parked in the driveway was not indicative of the presence of his mother at home, her cold welcome as he entered the kitchen was unmistakable.

« Ou est-ce que t'étais passe ? T'es parti depuis plus de deux heures. C'est ton choix mais ne pas appelé et laisser ton frère et ta sœur tout seul, je ne comprends pas. »

Barely able to formulate a response and answer, "I was going to be jus…," Stan was interrupted.

« Tout ce semestre c'est bien passé et c'est maintenant que tu décides d'être irresponsable ? » A question he knew she did not care for an answer. *« Tu sais très bien que je travaille plus d'heures tant que tes cours reprennent. Je ne sais pas ce que tu fabriques quand t'es pas a l'école, et dieu sait que ca te prend du temps de rentrer à la maison quand tu vas chez cette fille. Et ne pense pas que je ne suis pas au courant parce que ta sœur me raconte tout ! »* There, for a moment, seemed a smile, however fleeting, on her face.

Her silence was a chance for Stan to respond, perhaps he could find some exculpation as he was barely guilty, and only of the first count. "I, *j'étais juste avec Brent aujourd'hui. Il rentre chez lui demain et on voulait juste passer un peu de temps ensemble avant qu'il parte. »* His Creole may have been accent-challenged, but it seemed to melt his mother's face into a nascent understanding, an effect he did not consciously engineer and to which he was not averse. *« Pardon, je sais que t'étais partie depuis 5 minutes, »* referring to the time difference between his leaving the house and her arrival at home, *« mais j'aurais du t'avertir avant de partir. »*

Sighing, *« oh, mon cher, t'es un jeune homme et je sais bien que t'as des choses à faire. Je te soutiens pour tes cours d'été et c'était ton idée aussi, tu te souviens ? »*

« Je sais, » he inserted.

« Tu voulais la voiture alors j'en ai acheté une autre et tu voulais kotter parce que c'est plus facile pour toi d'étudier, surtout avec la médecine. Mais je dois travailler aussi moi et tu sais ca. On peut bien trouver un moyen pour que ca marche pour tous les deux, non ? »

« Oui, » his response was that of humility.

« Tu dis que tu veux être un cardiologue et entre le bon dieu, toi et moi, je sais que tu y arriveras. Tu sais que tout ce que je te souhaite c'est d'y arriver, juste ? »

« Oui maman, je sais. » The smile on his face was mutual.

« Je sais que tu sais mais parfois ca aide de le répéter. »
Moving to embrace her son, *« ne laisse plus ton frère et
ta sœur sans supervision quand je ne suis pas la,
compris, »* she hugged him. Stan's response was an
inaudible accord. *« Tu sais que tu es tout ce que j'ai, »*
she began.

« Oui je sais. T'es tout ce que j'ai aussi, » was Stan's
terse response.

She continued, *« et un jour je sais que tu vas me briser
le cœur mais c'est pas grave parce que tu seras un
cardiologue. »* In arms, but releasing the embrace, they
both laughed. *« Aide moi un peu avec la vaisselle parce
que je ne pense pas que personne ait mangé dans cette
maison aujourd'hui. Mais d'abord, raconte-moi un peu
au sujet de cette fille que ta sœur pense être ta petite
amie. »* His mother's inquiry was one to which he shook
his head, smiling, as he formed an argument. Standing at
the sink, the dishes Stan began washing reflected rays
from a sun, setting outside, whose temperature was not
as hot during late July.

Sept

Everything was as it should. The summer heat was soothing and the days, though longer, were too short for their beauty. Children seemed to spend more time outside than in, parents even opted to walk instead of drive, seeming to follow the example by their children. Yes, things were as they should, warmed up, but relaxed. While everything else around seemed to be relaxing or getting easier, there was a contrast in the social and ethical values in medicine class of PHI 337. In a course where the qualifications for humanity, what it meant fundamentally to be human, and other such related views that sought to define personhood, were argued, little was made in headway to any useful conclusions. Arguments for, on, or against criteria for characteristics such as death, consciousness, or life aside, Science 337 students argued for arguments, argued against arguments, argued with each other, and even argued against themselves, or so it seemed. The end to classes were altogether unhappy moments for students alike in that most, if not all, arguments could in one way and an other be refuted. Student arguments often began with objectively good intentions with respect to subject matter, with a sense of propriety. They could be observed in more ways than one with their many aspects such as great excitement in loudness and vociferousness. But more markedly, they were defined by refutations followed by momentary periods of tensed silence in considerations, and characterized most prominently by students' dignified despondence and, especially, startling brevity. But these were not major concerns for a couple students, especially one in particular.

The mind is a terrible place. The landscape of the intellectual and genius alike are not much different from that of which society would consider less than so, dim in wit, dull, or plainly stupid. In fact, any difference in the mental faculties of humanity could be described as "slight." And in the case of a criminal and the most magnanimous of us about, ostensibly polar opposites and extremes beyond the normal range as it were, it could be argued the two personalities can originate from the very same mind. But it is not for us to concern *our* mind with normalcy, or lack thereof, in view through social norms or psychological dogma. It is with the vicissitudes of the mind, that character of human psyche, to which we will focus our attention. How was it that the profound arguments held in class could stir most minds to leap into coloring arguments in exciting ways? The answer was immaterial, for to Stan the arguments paled in comparison to the dialogue between Maddie and him earlier that day. Only hours before, Maddie, although obviously or, perhaps, not so obvious, was iso-form, and had begun to transform in his construal of her person.

∼

It was Thursday, the last day of the month, and in that way turns go, it was Stan's responsibility for that day's drive. Having already decided with Maddie to drive on the second class-days of the week, Stan, however, was not ready. Having busied himself with chores, readings and writings, and drawing, he was hurried for time. Simultaneously, however impossible, writing the paper he knew was due that day and finishing his drawing, he could hear the sharp-water sound in, "time waits for no one," his mother's voice with its milkshake quality characteristic of her Haitian-Creole accent. He hurried to finish his paper, thinking to himself he needed more knowledge in behavioral sciences to understand why he was always rushed for time than to explain the reasoning behind adding as the title to the drawing his words of choice.

Anticipating, for certain, that he would receive a text from Maddie, he began to prepare his shoulder bag in the way that was usual. Putting to sleep his laptop-computer, Stan inserted this as the first item, followed by his flip-notebook, into the bag. His water bottle was next to be placed in the bag, along with a pack of gum. Having denied any oral fixation in the past, and as such quietly to himself, Stan knew any chew or edibles were integral to allowing him concentrate while working on interestingly boring matters such as reading or writing. The last of items to enter his backpack were his pens and pencils, and had Stan ever allowed his conscious mind take note of this, he may have obviated the alarmed moments he had, however infrequently, during tests or other such assessments when he would find he forgot or lost his writing utensils. Slinging the bag over his shoulder, he began his jog through the house to the side door through which he exited to his car. Another repression of mental matters prevented Stan from being aware, or perhaps acknowledging, the excitable feel he had on his way to Maddie's house; the thought of finishing his paper was enough to keep at bay "these feelings," he thought.

His arrival was of no consequence but quite different in that unusual way road kill is unusual, maybe even strange, but not surprisingly unexpected. Almost immediately, as he turned into her driveway, he began thinking of what to say to her when she entered the car. His thoughts were not racing, nor were they at ease, and finding his feelings, he tried to rationalize that of course there were bound to be some tension when any two people were to meet, even in the case of both being of the same sex. Thus, how much more this particular case? However, that instance was the fifth time they would ride together.

The moments were few as she began walking up the declivity that served as her driveway toward the car. Time seemed to speed by, for she was almost upon the vehicle, upon Stan as it were, and again Stan felt he was running out of time. He did not know whether to greet her in some way, or pose a question which was sure to put into her mouth a response that could buy him more time. But his thoughts were interrupted by her attempts to enter the car, which he promptly solved by unlocking the doors he painfully had been remiss in doing beforehand.

As she lowered herself into the cabin, Stan, with immediacy, "did you write your paper," posed his first question which to him, surprisingly, felt as the better option in beginning their conversation and, simultaneously, sojourn. Moving to reverse out into the road, Stan held an arm on the steering column, the other on the back side of the passenger seat, and turned his head to face the rear of the vehicle. His demeanor was not unlike that of a driving student under the careful scrutiny of a driving teacher or of a proctor under the conditions of a driver's test.

Because of this, "no, our paper is not due until Tuesday," Maddie's response which was conditioned with a smile that inflexed her tone, was missed, by way of body language by Stan. He did, however, catch the last of her upturned corners in eyes and mouth, which he noted by the response of his heart, for it neither fluttered, increased in rate of beats, nor dared the rumored arrest or cessation, but smiled in kind. Or were those *his* eyes and mouth? But having turned her attention from his countenance, Maddie missed his expression and not in part as he had done just moments before, but completely. As he deliberated the importance of his feelings, "why, did you do the paper already, again" she followed with her question.

"Yeah," he began, "and a little drawing too," he added hoping she heard the part. "I just have to reacquaint myself with the syllabus," and with a pause slightly more than slight, he continued, "it's really messing me up." It was perhaps the lack of another question that responses or answers failed to follow in conversation, and this marked the start of cessation in talk, but this was just as well.

The turns, three lefts and two rights, stop signs, three in total, and traffic lights, there were many in the town and it counted five that day, always fraught their transit. Along with the many automotive maneuvers necessary to enter high traffic on Transit road, navigating traffic made for a transpiration of different exchanges between the two. As language goes, there were tacit exchanges between Maddie and Stan, perhaps a dialogue between their subconscious that was not all together different from speech in conversation, or was it quite the same. The car would sway and veer in motion, and being the driver, Stan kept to the road with his attention.

Maddie, however, stole looks at his particulars. It was no thing new to her, finding what she liked in another, and doing so while not being particular about certain aspects such as the hair and how, if at all, it caressed the head. Eyes, whatever the color, as long as they were sharp but could soften with a smile. The neck, without vessels, but strong and leading to a prominent jaw. She observed these in Stan, but it was not that which caught her fancy. His profile told of a body well-cared for, and this she saw in his musculature, and posture. She detected a subtle outline of the flexor digiti muscles of his left arm, rested firmly on the steering column and passively tensed, while simultaneously regarding the extensor and toned pronator teres of his right, strongly gripping the gear shift as his arm rested on the console of the car.

Barely seeing his legs as they worked the pedals of the car, for the sun shone on his upper half, she could make out their outline which her memory filled with musculature and tone, and seeing the increasingly luminated parts of his body, as his thighs joined his trunk, she realized how angled his form was. He was either in a ninety- or forty-five degree angle depending on the joint, and his relaxed demeanor told of an experienced driver, though admittedly, she would have done with more speed. But all her observations aside, there was a feeling within her that she *shouldn't* be looking at him in that way, his muscles, his posture, his chest, which she was certain was barreled, as it heaved slowly out and in, down and up. This feeling along with her admiration for, of all things, his skin, which she found a brown tinged with what she would describe as bronze, for it had a metallic quality as if the underlying musculature were wrought with iron, yet had a glow to it. It seemed that the sun's rays, shining on it as they were, imbrued it with qualities that for reasons she could not conceive reminded her of puppies or kittens. Instinctively, she moved her gaze, now fully aware she was set on spying on him, to his lips which were… She stopped, looking at Stan that is, for having stopped at a light, he had turned his awareness to her, and feeling less abashed than guilty she refocused her attention on her notebook. If she felt any compunction, however brief, she was not alone in the feeling. After all, she was not alone in the spying on companions.

He smiled, "are you alright?" The light changed and he caught it in his periphery, "you seem like you have something on your mind," he continued. Was he referring to the looks he had caught her giving him earlier, or something else, he did not know for it was just a question.

However, neither did she, and that was the question. "Yeah, I'm fine," she started, "its just," she paused, "I wanted to tell you something."

Finding that she was waiting on him to respond, "really," he examined, "ok, what is it?" From her shoulder, where the seatbelt began, her clothing was smooth, in a way, caressing her body and smoothing from what he knew to be her deltoid muscle to the clip at her hip which he found to be suggestive when she walked. But it then held nothing except her thighs which were smoothed over by her skin-tight leggings. He had done so earlier and especially as she expected his attention, Stan again ran his eyes over her figure, catching the pink tank-top underneath her blouse which, along with the blouse and seatbelt, delineated her breasts. Following the seatbelt, and rolling from the smooth of her chest, he observed the wrinkled sections of the blouse which lay over her midsection and hinted at a fairly soft but firm abdominals. While he was aware that somewhere on that torso was a tattoo of her favorite artist, as she had informed him, its location was equal in question as to what it looked like. The way she took in a breath before speaking had him wonder, "…my God, why…," for he found it, not oddly, unusually attractive.

She continued, "well, it's not a big deal. I know I said before he wasn't well, but I just wanted you to know that today, a month ago, my grandfather had a stroke."

There was a pause they both understood to be for the purpose of respect, and then Stan replied, "yeah," he began, "and I imagine it feels like it happened yesterday," he stated, hoping he was correct or even close. Stan, turning to her, asked, "he's not, dead or dying is…"

"Oh, no, he's fine," she answered. "I mean, alive," smiling dryly. A car had passed, and she looked out the window. "Yep," she sighed, turning back, she smiled and continued, "but it doesn't help having this class which reminds me of hospitals and healthcare." He listened for an opening, but she was not finished, "and I know I still want to be a nurse, but right now I don't need to think about that," she paused, "you know," less a question than a statement as she sought his face for agreement.

To this he was aware, "yeah, I know, nobody needs to go through that *and* this at the same time." Stan soon became aware, perhaps too quickly, of his role in the conversation. He felt she was becoming more comfortable with him and conversing. Certainly, he was with her.

"And did I tell you about the sociology class I'm taking also," she posed as though she were not expecting an answer. Stan, in quick pretense, made as though he were thinking, shook his head as he activated his procerus muscle, furrowing his brow. He bit his lip and prepared to respond at which point Maddie reentered, "because," she paused, for Stan, trying hard to sell his pretense or perhaps just fulfilling his role in the conversation, had squeezed in a "no." She continued, but with something of a new or reset mindset, "well, because my teacher for that class does not give me proper instructions," she argued, "every time I turn in an assignment the way he wants it done, he continues to give me poor grades." Seeming reinvigorated, Maddie would not seem to stop, and coming upon a red light, Stan reduced the car's speed to zero. "The worst part is, he continues to give me good reviews for my papers, but when it comes to the grades, he is screwing me."

Seeing this as a serious point to her, Stan entered by sympathizing, "so you're taking another class, that sucks," and followed by asking, "on what days is it?"

"Oh, it's not a," she trailed off, thinking on what she wanted to say, "it's an online course you know, so I don't have to go in, which is good, but," she repositioned, "it is killing me, and I need it for my requirements."

Wanting to help in as little a way possible, after all he could not rid Maddie of her problems, Stan responded, "this is all very stress-inducing for you." He looked to switch lanes, "I mean, it's stressing me," they looked to each other and smiled, and he suggested, "I know I've told you before, but you have to de-stress. It's really bad for your health, especially your heart." Stan was no stranger to stress, and he knew as well as any other how to deal with it. Often employing such methods as measuring his heart rate manually or closing his eyes and listening to hear it beat to gauge pressure, he knew of certain ways to measure stress, or in this case distress. But he also knew that to help her feel better he needed to throw the ball back in her court while simultaneously pushing her focus to something less distressing. "Have you told Frank," he asked.

Having taken Kensington Expressway some of the way, they were fast approaching an intersection. Stan made to slow down, taking the right lane in preparation to turn, and slowing to an almost complete stop. He looked both ways for traffic as though it were possible for traffic to come by their way, from the passenger side, in the right lane he intended to enter. Stan circled the wheel clockwise, gave the car gas, and as it rolled onto the road he looked over to Maddie, awaiting her response.

It seemed she too was watching for incoming traffic from both sides of the lane, but in catching his gaze, she started, "you know you're the worst driver right?" She was smiling, much to Stan's desire, and began more cheerfully, "you could have taken the thruway, and not only could we have gotten here faster," at this point they both were smiling for they knew how she liked driving fast and passing others on the thruway. But she digressed, almost catching him off-guard, "yeah," she dragged out, "I told him." Somehow he knew there was something she was not telling him, whether it was about classes or her grandfather, perhaps her friend, he did not know. But he also felt she was making her way to divulging something. "We were actually walking my dog on Friday," she restarted, "funny story actually," she assured him. "Yeah, we were walking along the bike path, and Frank decided to go off and pee at a bush," she continued, and he could tell this was not a serious recount as her tone had changed from that of a young woman to the thin and airy sound characteristic of insincere and almost artificial talk. "Well," she dragged, "my dog decided that she would run after him, or at least I thought she was running *after* him."

Stan felt glad she was "feeling" better, but was admittedly bruised by the thought she was holding back by not telling him what really was on her mind, but feigning genuine interest, asked, "the beagle, right?"

"Yeah, my *little* beagle," she smiled, "so she ran after him, or so I thought until he walked away calling her but she stood there sniffing his piss," she laughed. Stan, unsure, smiled. "Listen," she urged, "that's not all, because as we stood calling her, and I even ran after her calling 'Lexi,' Pedro Dams ran right by us and said, 'hey Maddie' to me." And as she recalled she looked for his attention, "you remember him, he ran for our school and now goes to Cornell, right," making it less a question and more a statement. Although she did not look, Stan nodded in agreement. "I remember thinking how good his body looked, you know, he wasn't wearing a shirt, and of course Frank agreed with me," she continued, "and I felt like such a weirdo because my dog was being difficult. And worse, all Frank and I did was stand there and stare at him as he ran by." She softened, "at least Frank said 'hey', and now that I think of it, I think he seems to like you too," she added as an after note.

Stan turned into the Main-Jefferson lot and this signified their arrival, and in the way of Stan's driving rituals, he proceeded to take off his seatbelt. Maddie noticed this, and she too took off her seatbelt, and moved to gather her notebook and other belongings. Finding and pulling into a parking space Stan looked to Maddie, and before he could utter the words of instruction she looked to him, and as though she understood, reached for *his* bag as well. He smiled and put the car on park as he turned the volume on the radio up as it had been turned down earlier, given their conversation, but was left on. He thanked her for grabbing his pack as he pushed the power button, turning off the radio, and shut off the car. She nodded in acknowledgement. Wasting little time in posing the question he held on with as soon as she had finished her last sentence, he asked, "does he really, Frank I mean, 'cause I thought he has a boyfriend right now?" Stan was not fond of Frank or any other homosexual, and although he was not threatened in any way by Frank he did seem a little troubled at the time.

Watching him as she handed him his bag, she answered, "yeah, he does, but you remember what I told you about his boyfriend." She recounted, "he sometimes goes the other way, with girls, and he tells me that in the case his boy left," watching him ill at ease, she positioned, "he would love to," she trailed off, laughing. She had watched Stan's demeanor and found him uncomfortable, and so had made to play a joke on him.

"What," he asked, looking to see what could possibly be the source of her amusement, and feeling her shoulder on his elbow as he made to place his bag on his shoulders, he realized it was the first time he had "made contact" with her.

Seemingly, she did not notice for she continued, "you," she chuckled. "I know you don't see it, but you look so weirded-out right now," she continued, repositioning, "I mean, you're so paranoid." He was glad she was having her joke on him but, her antics and his objections aside, what he really wanted to know was just under the surface, he felt. However, before he could dig deeper into her, he noticed a classmate sitting at one of the tables to the left of the doors as they entered the antechamber portion of the REWSC.

Signaling with their arms to their classmate, the two walked as though their gait were rehearsed, with Maddie in front and Stan slightly behind. As they approached the square table, there sat a strikingly plain lady with a wiry frame clad in chic fashion and with red-tinged brunette hair in a bun, who threw them a thin smile. Her tender expression seemed to dance along with her head which balanced on a long neck angled with her narrow but square shoulders. As Stan made to introduce them, "hey, do you remember us from class," he could not shake the thought that he was neither attracted to, nor repulsed by her.

"Yes, you're Stan, right," she acknowledged. He nodded a yes, but being certain of his response she moved to greet Maddie as well, "and you're Jenny," she intoned with a hint of interrogation.

Maddie was not offended as well as Stan could tell, but he measured a hint of displeasure in her correction, "no, Maddie, I'm Maddie." Finalizing their greetings and doing with niceties, Maddie and Stan joined Cecile in preparing for the test they had only hours away. As Stan sat he again thought, how was it possible that he could not touch on one thing, perhaps it were many a thing, that presented his classmate in such an austere light. No longer thinking of Cecile, he traced back his thoughts and, remembering what he had earlier wanted to ask Maddie, turned his attention her way. He found, naturally he supposed, Maddie engaged in conversation with their classmate, and although he wanted to get to what Maddie was holding back, knew the time was not right. And the time had to be perfect.

Maddie left her belongings with Stan as she left to get her favorite beverage, and to Stan, "you want anything," she asked.

"Uh, yeah." Stan did not expect she would be willing to accommodate him, "whatever you're having."

Watching her as she left for the Commons, Cecile and Stan sat without much looking at each other, or saying a word. As such, there was an awkward quiescence after Maddie left that ended only after Cecile asked, "so how long have you known her?"

"Maddie," he asked, knowing full well whom they were talking of, "a long time, I guess. I mean, I knew her before, but it's like I'm getting to know her for real now."

Cecile smiled, "I can see that, but you'll learn as you go." If Stan was confused by her statement, he did not show it.

~

The lecture topic for the previous week had been on the criteria by which death is determined, and so the discussion by the classmates was on this very subject. "So you're saying that brain-death is the criteria for death," Cecile asked in a way that seemed she did not really know the answer, and worse, did not seem to have her own opinion.

"*I* don't say that, he does," replied Stan, referring to the philosopher of interest.

The back and forth exchange between Cecile and Stan seemed to irritate Maddie for she voiced her desire to move on to another argument, "guys, we've gone over this twice already, let's move on to the dicephalic twins thought experiment." This move looked to the idea that one was *not* one's body, and though they may own it, are not themselves within it. This served to relay the concept of death as complete once that, however undefined, part of the person died or in certain implications, was killed. This general move toward the cerebrum excited Stan for he was interested in the concept of the person, you, being housed only in your mind. A thought amongst impulses, an idea in reality.

"Ok, let's look at the cerebral transplant thought experiment now," Stan prompted, and though he was excited to look at this aspect of their upcoming test, truthfully, he knew himself to be interested mostly in the concept of such a procedure and its outcomes rather than its implications with respect to defining the location of personhood, and its termination by that location's cessation of functions. To be able to look through an other's eyes, smell by their nose, and utilize their other senses, not to mention motor functions as well, was an idea all too potentially charged for Stan to ignore or fully entertain as well. But on a lower level, or smaller scale, that concept is what Stan was consciously trying with Maddie. At times, he wondered if she were not doing the same to him, but with greater delicacy and finer subtlety.

Soon the discussion relaxed from studying on subject to being more a conversation about different subjects. Maddie was rapt by conversation with Cecile and she must have found their exchange pleasurable for anyone, Stan included, could detect the mollified countenance she wore. Feeling less interested than useless, Stan searched for his phone in his pockets, and finding it, checked for messages and voicemails to which he promptly responded. To the text-messages that is, for he neglected the voicemails. It was not long before snippets of conversation, which otherwise may have been filtered uninteresting by Stan, caught his attention.

"And where are those," Cecile posed, and she seemed to have her opinions of the locales on what she had inquired this time.

"Ok, so I have a monster tattoo, and it's on this side," showed Maddie as she pulled on the sentence a bit, pointing to and patting her right buttocks. "But the piercing," she again dragged as though she were setting up for a punch line, but then followed with a terse phrase, "is on my clit."

Taken by surprise but avoiding it show, Cecille slightly thrust her head forward, toward Maddie, as she made to ask, "on your…" she trailed off in that smiling-question way, while gesturing toward Maddie's privates.

Nodding an acknowledgement as though she were undulating, Maddie responded, "yep."

Also taken by surprise, but utilizing fewer defense mechanisms to conceal it, Stan was sure he had been informed by Maddie of her piercing for she had told him of the tattoo. Failing to remember, he was also sure it was the only other piercing she carried, and as such he set to think and remember, but not before Cecile posed, "did it hurt? I mean, does it hurt?"

Fully aware of Stan, perhaps through her other senses than vision, Maddie was sure to show no signs of distress or discomfort. After all she was not troubled for she wanted Stan to hear that truthfulness he knew him to speak of before, and which she thought he either greatly liked or intensely disliked. "No, it didn't hurt really, and it doesn't hurt now," but to condition her sentence, she added, "it's like a part of me now, although I can feel it sometimes, especially when I cross my legs."

"Does he know," Cecile indicated whom she had inquired about with her eyes.

"Does who, Stan," Maddie asked in return, "why would he…"

"Oh," gasped Cecile. With her right hand she covered her mouth, and with the left she extended to meet Maddie's arm. "I thought the two of you were together," she confessed.

Stan was fully aware of the situation, and as Maddie made to answer Cecile, she looked at him. Nonchalantly, "no," she responded.

"So the two of you carpool together just as friends," she asked, and waiting for no answer, Cecile looked at Stan, "so what happens when you're ready to leave and she's not?"

"I dunno. I mean, what am I going to do, tell her am out of here and begin walking?" Stan's reply resulted in an eruption of laughter and Maddie, in particular, chortled, "ahaha… oh… I love you." A comment none other than Stan sat very well to hear.

Cecile continued to probe, "so, who has the better car, in your opinion," looking at the both of them.

Maddie answered as Stan was reluctant to make the no-less true but potentially hurtful statement, "he does. He has a really nice Toyota sedan."

"Ooh, rich boy," Cecile began to say.

Stan practiced modesty, "it's only a Corolla, it's not like it's a Lexus or something."

"Yeah, but what year," Cecile continued.

"Twenty-twelve," Stan admitted.

Expressing confirmation with her hands and neck, Cecile reacted, "like I said, rich boy."

"Hardly," Stan began to protest, but Cecile was unfinished.

"I bet you also live in a fancy neighborhood," Cecile again assumed, this time incorrectly.

Stan, again, began to voice his dissent but he was slower than Maddie, "actually I live in a way nicer neighborhood than he does," she assured.

"Ok, girlfriend," returning her full attention to Maddie, and it was not long before they resumed their previous distraction. Cecile seemed genuinely interested for she was now fascinated, and continuing in her inquisition, asked, "you know, it's something I hear, but, can't you," she paused for what did not seem to have a dramatic purpose but, all the same, gave the effect, "you know, get off that way?" But it was not Cecile alone who found

Maddie's response piquant, or saw the entire conversation as intriguing. Stan was just as interested in the girls' conversation, and he found most appealing Maddie's ability to be so open with someone whom he considered the perfect stranger. She presented no threat physically or, more importantly, socially, and yet she embodied a source of interesting reactions in both him and Maddie. As Maddie prepared her objections to what she found to be hearsay, the group was interrupted by another classmate; a tall Jordanian lady whose origin was given away not by her countenance, which seemed less Arabic, but by her hijab which flowed to join her dress. An image which, quite peculiarly, reminded Maddie of baby bottles. The introduction of a new classmate was also the reintroduction of their possible test topics, and a level of focus that almost resembled work. Because class would begin less than thirty minutes later, their time was used more wisely.

~

Science 337 students knew that the test was not going to be administered right away. In fact, most took comfort in being able to simultaneously review their notes while listening to and participating in class lecture. This was to be their third test and the students had already become comfortable with the way the class was conducted, and so felt relaxed enough to participate in class discussions while making arguments. Again the criteria for death was analyzed with a greater emphasis on organ procurement, determining the point, or points, by which organs could be taken from bodies was significant as the topic of the day. As views and arguments for when a body was no longer functioning as a whole, or when the person no longer was in the living grew, it was not inconceivable to come to a point where what one *could* do with their organs while they had control, a courtesy of life, resulted in the posing of such questions as, "can you sell your organs?" Ostensibly, it seemed, one could sell their organs. After all, it was *their organs*. But the ramifications of such a reality went beyond the possibilities in criminality, and went even as far to question the value and definition of personhood. This, however, is of little matter for there, almost always, was a period of silence that ensued such moments where profound, or seemingly so, questions were posed by the instructor to the students. And, in few cases, a point in question was broached by a student.

Following the next question and consideration from instructor to students, "can you sell yourself into slavery, or prostitution," was such a period which Maddie seized to whisper to Stan her thoughts. He was surprised at the injection of her voice into his ear, which was just as well for her voice in whisper was as he imagined silk-steel would sound, pulled taught and played as a note. She had seemed singularly focused on the class discussions, and although, as usual, she did not say anything, he thought her note-taking and attention to be a result of her focus. "I don't know, I mean, I think you *can* sell yourself into prostitution," and she trailed off as though she had more to add, but with class discussion descending from the level that would rouse interests in her monologue, she cut the whisper.

It was not long after the policies regarding organ procurement, such as opting in or out and presumed consent which, interestingly enough, was routine salvaging, that the test was administered. And time seemed short for it was soon that Stan was stating, "I think I did very well on that test," to Maddie who responded in kind, "me too."

The two were alone as they walked out of the classroom. Alone again as they made their way down the stairs to exit the building which left them to the company of the night and that feeling one gets walking through a well-lit parking lot that retained its dark spots. Stan was aware of their moments together, and seeing this one in particular as his opportunity to pry her to the core, he tempered his desire with time, waiting. But if Stan thought he were the only of the two to have inquiries, he would soon find himself on the receiving end of Maddie's questions. As the two entered Stan's car, they noticed one of their classmates enter her car, and while this may have otherwise been of no significance, the make and model of the vehicle quickly took up as subject matter for the first leg of their drive home. At some point Maddie had informed Stan she thought some and certain others, referring to the students in their class, were much older than they were. But given that the exact ages were unknown, and a range was indeterminable, the two surmised that given one of their classmates was exiting a parking space in a "Mercedes MLK, 4matic," as Stan had informed Maddie as they closely followed the vehicle, that their classmates were easily three to five, and maybe even *seven*, years their elders.

However, car-talk notwithstanding, Maddie began at first talking about the test and her thoughts on it. "I'm glad she had for the second question those thought experiments having to do with the cerebrum," she began, "that, to me, was the easiest of the four questions to answer."

Sooner or later, he thought, he would ask her. But if she wanted to speak on the test now, so be it, "yeah, me too," he replied. "I really liked that question, but I also felt the rest of the test wasn't too bad."

Because his subconscious must have really wanted to get to what mattered, he turned up the radio as he turned it on, but not before Maddie, who must have traced her thoughts back to what she had told him earlier in class, restarted by asking, "do you know why I thought selling one's self into prostitution was fine?" She took note of his actions, "why do you listen to all these stations," she asked, seeming more annoyed than inquisitive. "You know, I notice when you're not listening to your jazzy music, you turn to this NPR station."

To this Stan thoughtfully responded, "a friend of mine introduced me to it during the second semester, and in listening I found that they have good programming and address interesting topics." Knowing she was not particularly interested, but seemed to be asking about that station in particular, he continued, "I liked it. And no, I don't know why, but what *I* want to ask," he inflexed and, thinking the time no better, asked, "is about you and your family."

She stabbed him with her eyes, and following a momentary but painless silence, she answered in question, "what about me and my family?"

Stan was not sure what he wanted to know and so did not know where to have her start. But he knew to get something, anything from her that may hint at her true distress, he had to start somewhere. "Well, I know more about your friends and relationships than I do about your family. For example, I don't know how many siblings you have, if any, there are usually three or more cars in your driveway, you know," he realized he was going on and on, and although this was enough to have her start, he knew he needed a stronger point. "Start with your parents," he urged.

The silence that followed was neither terrible nor soothing for there was a tension that was evident even as she began, "ok, ok," in a manner that indicated she was reaching to find how to place her words. "Um, ok, when my parents had me they weren't married," she told, "my grandparents weren't happy, especially on my mom's side," she assured him, "so they soon after must have gotten hitched because when I was five they divorced. Now my mom is remarried, and with the exception of my stepbrother, I have no siblings," she informed, answering the point on siblings Stan had earlier brought up. She also added, "and as you know, I live with my dad who likes cars, but I do often visit my mom." Stan felt she had done him a favor, so when she asked, "anything else," he shook her a "no" with his head. The silence that ensued was filled with a mile of the sound from the sixty-mile per hour engine, and a radio report on the increase in cyber attacks. She sighed. "I'm hungry," she warmed the cold silence, "and I'm out of pop, I need more caffeine," she joked.

"I'm not stopping at Tim Hortons for you to feed your caffeine addiction," he smiled, hoping she would catch it.

When she smiled in kind, "I know, it's just that for someone who always talks of de-stressing, that was, you know," he was not sure what she was getting to, but if his intuition was of any use, her opinion on the now passed moment was his favorable conjecture, "weird. I mean you wanting to know about my family out of nowhere," she admitted, "it took me by surprise." Further revealing, "I would have thought you would want to know about my piercing or what my tattoo looked like, or something, but not that," a pause, "my family," she quipped sarcastically and they both laughed. He knew her to be honest but, admittedly, was surprised once again by her directness and pleasant poignancy.

With this, their exchanges had again heated up to conversation, and feeling more comfortable, Maddie reminded him, "so do you know why," she asked as though he were fully aware of what she had in mind.

"Do I know why," he dragged, "what?"

As if to guide him through his memories for he apparently could not find his way back, "in class, I told you I thought that selling yourself into prostitution should be fine," she recounted. "And I want you to guess why I said that, why I think that," she challenged. Maddie was painfully aware that Stan had not considered what she had earlier told him in class as having a bearing beyond the class discussion, and that he must have put it out of his mind as he did the time she had told him she too never slept in a real bed. But Stan was more aware than she could have known for he considered the thought that what she had to say would have significance with respect to what could be eating her internally. Making a turn from one highway to another, he determined in his face to show thoughtful interest in what she had broached. Although, his look could easily have been perceived as concentration to a turn where accidents were not uncommon.

As the car turned Maddie must have been under greater influence by inertia, or so it seemed. For she turned with the car as to have her back side, the area that served as the origin for her gluteus maximus and erector spinae muscles, pushed against the door. Her left hip was angled into the seat sharply but softly as it served to support her right side which rested on it and, as such, her entire anterior, a vulnerable gesture had Stan considered the implications of all her vital organs being exposed, was pointed at him. Successfully navigating the turn back on to Transit road, Stan turned to look at Maddie as she indubitably was about to fill him in. What he saw was not Maddie, but a beauty in a beast, the darling in the *monster*, for light from an oncoming car illuminated her right cheek and played across a cyan iris which at that moment transformed from a ring to a disc, and the sensation her colored silhouette gave along with her parted lips in mid utter was not a chill down his spine, but rather up it, terminating in his face with a tingling of his cheeks.

She surely, "because," and slowly admitted, "I was once paid a hundred dollars by this one guy to have sex with him." By now Stan was familiarized with what seemed to be her never-ending, shocking revelations. But taking it as a shock, nonetheless, he knew the better of things to do and threw her a look that was less surprise and more encouragement for her to continue. "I mean, we had slept together once before, and it wasn't that great, at least for me, you know," she continued as he listened, "so he wanted another go at it," she dragged, "but he offered a hundred dollars so I felt it made up for, you know, his deficit, so I took it." Stan did not know how she felt after *that* revelation, and as such, he wondered. Choosing not to ask her as he did not want to offend her, however impossible, he was appreciative of her freeness in sharing the thought and experience with him as he imagined he may not have been the only person aware of this, but was sure he counted in the few.

He smiled. "What," she asked. Sensing her playful inquisition, he made sure to respond in the least judgmental way possible. He responded, "I'm," he paused to consider his words, "just glad you felt comfortable to share that with me," he conditioned, "I mean that is really something personal to admit to anyone," and ending, "and of all people, me."

If Maddie was not uncomfortable before, she certainly was at that point for she turned back to her usual position and, in fact, proceeded to put her knees up to the dashboard as she slunk backward into the seat. "Oh, you know, I just wanted you to know," she confided, "I mean, I feel like, you know how you look at things differently, I feel the same way." Maddie noticed they were passing the last of the many car dealerships on Transit before their turn into a town road that would eventually take them to her home. "I just don't feel that you shouldn't be able to do what you want, especially when you have the explicit freedom and nothing is threatened, you know," she asked but not expecting an answer. "And I'm not saying anything along the lines of murder, that you should be able to get away with it or anything like that," and making sure to condition, "as long as you don't threaten anyone else, whether physically or by other means, and you have to know that once you do something, you can't take it back, you know." Stan was content in biding time as he allowed her express her thoughts, for he also had his own he wanted to share. But again, he knew the timing to be inappropriate. She looked to him awaiting his attention, which given, shared, "like I know we didn't used to talk, but now that we're friends," she made her point, "it's a decision that we both made, and now we can't take it back." They both laughed. "Also, I'm sorry about earlier today. Um, I didn't mean to make it sound like you live in the ghetto or something," she added.

Without looking at her, "oh, it's Ok," and throwing up his shoulders when he did, "besides, it wouldn't have been you to lie. After all," he added, "your neighborhood is nicer than mine."

As Stan made a left turn onto Maddie's street, it was the first time during their transit that he thought there had to be an end to their night. Feeling much the same way, Maddie began the end to their travel together by reminding Stan of the conversation they had in the driveway the night she took him to his house when she last drove. "Hey, I wanted to talk more about what we were discussing last week when I dropped you off." Stan remembered the conversation as well as he did the driveway on which he turned into, novel and familiar; dark, but given the street lamp, lit by view-points and, like the car's headlamps, when given a directed focus, revealed a larger picture in time. Stan was sure that given their time together and the history of their conversations the night was not going to end abruptly, but not wanting to assume or make any further guesses given his intuition, he slowed the wheels to a stop in the middle of her lengthy driveway. She waited as he put the car in park, and when he turned to look at her she began, "because I was thinking on what we said, especially what you said about everyone being the same, basically." She again repositioned in that way that placed her back to the door, giving Stan her full direction as the position freed both her arms which she used to gesticulate.

"Yeah," he responded questioningly, indicating he wanted her to continue with her query.

"Well, I just wanted to, you know, with respect to sinning, know if it really was the same," she considered a moment, "you know, with lying and disobeying your parents, and, and all those things you said."

Aware it was his turn to enter, but realizing the gravity of the shared thoughts, he considered his words carefully, "well, yeah, I mean obeying your parents is right there along with not killing in the Ten Commandments, and people do that all the time. Well, less murdering, even though there is such a thing as spiritual killing, and more disobeying" and with assurance, added, "besides the only difference between you and me is that I'm a virgin. Jesus talked with, hung out with, and healed tons of people whom I'm sure did worse things than have sex," to which Maddie smiled.

Responding, "well sex isn't bad," she dragged, "I would know," they laughed. "It's just that I did it before the whole getting married thing," she added, conditioning the statement. Stan came to realize that it was less the truth behind what was turning out to be a lengthy conversation, and more his willingness and desire to keep it going that had him shut off the radio and reduce the air to the first level. Something similar, if not all together the same, must have crossed Maddie's mind as she reached across, over Stan's arm resting on the center console, and shut off the idle engine whose din had seemed to suddenly invade their conversation as the car struggled against the decline.

"But you know," she again began, propping herself with the shoulder she rested between the top of the seat and headrest on which she steadied her head, "sex is not the only thing I sometimes feel guilty about." Stan had assumed that as Maddie was confident in her sexuality she did not feel guilt, and although she had conditioned her last sentence with "sometimes," he felt that she had her reservations about certain other things as well. After all, he thought, she thought it inappropriate to have extra-relational relationships given that she had a boyfriend. She continued, "I mean, I don't have any *qualms*," she dragged in cordially mocking him, "like you say, about sex, or even porn usually, and I think it's less about everyone else and more about me with these things," to which he nodded, and taking it as his gesture of understanding, she sought more, "you know what I mean?"

Stan was beginning to unfold the fabric that was Maddie, he was beginning to see the intricacies that added texture to *her* picture, and as he began to understand, he also felt he had to be careful and tempered in his responses. He wanted to state his points and share his views but without overstepping and treading on her exposed underbelly, so to speak. Or, trespass into any areas of her insecurities. "Well, like I've said, it's really not my place to, or anybody's for that matter," he remembered, "to say or decide what another person should or can do."

Stan was not sure if anything he was saying was getting across, made sense, or was right, but he did not much think on this. "You know, I come from a lot of love so I know that children can be told what to do by their parents because their parents love and care for them." He continued, "when they're children that is," he conditioned, "because like everyone else, including adults, children don't know jack until they know," further explaining, "but unlike adults, children don't always understand things, even what they know." She knew he was on a roll as he continued, "so, that's basically judging I think, and most people who do that don't really help the person they talk about because they never actually tell them. Besides, without my mom and all she means to me I'd probably be a sex fiend," he held back a smile as Maddie snickered, "or a drug lord, or underground hacker." They both laughed. Stan's highly hypothetical conjectures were interesting, however unlikely.

Maddie was sure of Stan's convictions, she saw his point of view and his reason. She was not averse to what he said and, in fact, she would have agreed with much if not all he said. But what she really wanted to know was what *he* thought about her, what his true opinions were on her. So, as if he had read her mind, Stan asked, "and you wanna know what *I* think?"

Almost involuntarily, Maddie responded with a sure, "yeah," and Stan smiled unexpectedly as he revealed, "I think you shouldn't do some of those things given their social weight." He did not watch for her reaction, so missed her abashed-grimace, but admitted, "even though it's not really taboo to have sex today. I mean, that's why I stopped dating because there seems to be some tacit expectation." They both smiled to each other, and he followed with, "but what I really think is that you can do whatever you want with your body if you think it's yours," giving her a look which she took as reference to some of the more philosophical of class considerations. She was mistaken, for he alluded to the first letter from Paul to the church of Corinth. Specifically, the last verses in the sixth chapter.

To finish, "but what *I* think doesn't matter because it's what you do that does, you know," he added, "whether you decide to do it on your own, with or by *your*self, or with God." Stan was feeling, at this point, very philosophical and he even considered quoting to Maddie Aristotle's, "what it lies in our power to do, it lies in our power not to do," with respect to his thoughts on people having the power to do good as well as evil by others, but he refrained, practicing brief speech. Maddie seemed to better understand Stan and his views though she would not consider informing him, especially as she remembered he had said something about abstaining from sex because his body, mind, and soul belonged to God the last time they had such a talk. But she had some unrelenting question to ask him.

"Um," finding some word difficulty, "I don't know why I'm feeling so self-conscious," Maddie informed Stan, "but I wanted, I want to know if you want to do something tomorrow, or sometime this weekend?" She tried not to avoid his eyes, but with little success.

"You mean, like hang out?"

"No, I mean like a date," the hint of sarcasm from Maddie went completely undetected by Stan.

"A date," he inquired.

"No, I'm kidding," she assured. "I don't know, just hanging out. I don't have school, I know you don't have school, and I want to go camping."

"Camping?"

"Just say yes," she commanded, "please," pleading.

"Alright," Stan agreed, "as long as it's after 6 tomorrow, I'm good. When do we plan on hanging, or will this be Saturday?"

"Ok. Um, we can work the details out later. You have a Facebook, right," she pretended not to know, but acknowledged his nodded response all the same.

Within Stan's awareness, but without Maddie's given her position in the cabin, was the fast closing front door to her house which must have been ajar moments before. When did that door open? How long had they sat together in the car? Time stood still, or so it seemed, and the image of the two in the car was a live-still, as if painted by Basil Hallward.

"You know," Maddie knew she did not have to express her comfort, or do so in the manner she chose as she twisted her arms about as pretzel dough and gave in her full pretense of girlish coy, "I, like talking to you," she smiled.

He responded in kind with a terse, "me too," smiling in return. Within the same minute, he was rolling backwards in the car, their goodbyes already said.

Huit

me: people suck

 Sent at 12:14 PM on Friday

Stan: Hey, you figured out the chat function...

me: yes its weird

Stan: How so?

How so, again for both comments

me: idk its just different that its here

and people suck because i have to do a peer review for my sociology class and it was due last night and i have yet to hear from my partner and i'm not doing so hot with it.

In short, the room was ornate. It was a chamber for sleeping and, perhaps, studying, though it can be imagined with little difficulty that little of that was going on at the time. The king-sized bed was hugged by perhaps the most comfortable of comforters, the design of which complemented, along with the sheets of the bed, the theme of the walls and the frieze on them. The commode was to Frank's right, guarding the window. Shying from the window to his left was the wood-glass computer table and its chair, which Maddie, occupied by the latest Apple desktop computer, occupied. The carpeting or, more appropriately, rug, for it was on hardwood flooring, its design along with the reddish-brown of the flooring complemented the mahogany frames of the pictures in Frank's room. And the framed pictures, however few for they numbered three in total, were placed two to the left, and the last to the right. Certainly holding some value for their owner, it was the final and fourth picture, placed on the far wall, that must have held great significance. Without a frame, interestingly, it was the image of several juxtaposed Victoria's Secret models, unclad but "covered." Reasons for why he would have such a picture would be highly speculative.

"Stop turning down my music, you're not the only one who is trying to concentrate," Frank admonished.

Maddie barely made to turn and face him when she responded, "you mean you concentrate better with the music on than off," scoffing, "since when?"

"Since this is my room, that's since when," retorted Frank.

The rapping on the keys along with her mouthing some of her comments preceded her response, "what, you're so corny sometimes."

"You're so gay," Frank knew this response to usually guarantee her full attention. Furrowing her brow and squinting for effect, she turned to face him, but said nothing. A surprise to Frank, but nothing that would have him relent.

Stan: was it you who didn't do it, or your partner who didn't do it?

why does your thing continue to go offline?

me: i cant do it because my partners paper isnt finished si she didnt send it

Stan: wait, are you using your phone right now?

me: no, i'm on a computer

Stan: Hmm, so then it's not your fault, also, did you send your partner your paper?

me: yes

i did

but i cant finish without her review

though it probably wont be helpful

 Sent at 12:20 PM on Friday

Stan: Hmm... I suppose your assessment was just as well. "People do suck."

me: and i'm a total black sheep my family doesn't love me I don't think.

so i've just decided that i'm going to adopt a fuck the whole world attitude and i'm going to be a hardcore bitch and i'm done with bs

Sent at 12:24 PM on Friday

Stan: what are you talking about?

me: i'm having a total meltdown of epic proportions lol

Sent at 12:26 PM on Friday

Stan: Oh, again? Maddie, you have to take care of yourself. YOURSELF, first, before you worry about others, whether you're genuinely worried about them, taking care of them in special ways, or worried about what they think of you.

Stress, is not healthy. Whether it's external (stress) or internal (distress).

me: i am basically mad at everyone that i know and i sent that girl a nasty email i don't even care anymore

Sent at 12:29 PM on Friday

Stan: clarify it by letting her know you're angry with her, and give your reason(s). Don't just be angry, anger is best used to good, not wasted on one's self.

me: i should totally keep a journal

Sent at 12:33 PM on Friday

Stan: You should, especially if it helps. It's always good to reflect too, imagine if and when you do away with all (most) of your stress(es) and can focus on life.

Sent at 12:35 PM on Friday

Stan: You mentioned everyone you know, "everyone"? I think there is a reason you mentioned that, and it's up to you to figrue out why. Anyway, you're not angry with me cause we're still "hanging out" today, right?

Sent at 12:40 PM on Friday

me: yeah we're still hanging out, we're going to olive garden

Stan: olive garden? I've never been there, and I actually wanted to go to a different place

me: why, the more reason we should go, and i can't believe you've never been there, you're so deprived

Stan: I really want to go this place near where my lab is

Stan: besides, nextt time we'll go wherever you want

me: fine, is your place a restaurant?

Stan: of course

me: do they have nice food?

Stan: Yes

me: is it nice, forget this, tell me where we're going

Sent at 12:42 PM on Friday

Stan: No. It will be a surprise…

me: Oh, Stan, that's romantic. And there will be a next time, and i get to choose, how romantic

Sent at 12:44 PM on Friday

Stan: romantic?

me: i was just kidding

Stan: you know you don't seem like the kidding type

me: i know, I'm not. but you know what is though, i couldn't help but notice on thursday that as we were getting ready to leave and you were getting your stuff that you were wearing boner shorts

Sent at 12:50 PM on Friday

Stan: boner shorts? what are you talking about…

me: you know, those nvm, i guess i really am not funny, forget it

Stan: If you say so.

me: ok, we're going camping on saturday, right/

me: ?*

Stan: yeah, about that. Where are we going to "camp" and for how long because I can't do sunday, and I definitely can't do today… so that leaves just saturday. Unless you want to go camping for one day…

Stan: hello?

Stan: Heloooo

 Sent at 12:59 PM on Friday

It seemed Maddie must have turned Frank's music off entirely, and as such Frank was beside himself. "Turn it back on you witch," he commanded.

Shocked, Maddie launched herself from the chair towards Frank and onto the bed, but not before she threw a pencil at him. The pencil glanced off the side of the then tent-like comforter, under which was Frank. Struggling against her weight and efforts, Frank was dangerously close to being overpowered by Maddie who incessantly struck at him with the pillow in her hand.

"Take it back," she struggled. "I said take it bc…," she stopped mid imperative as her attention was held by Frank's phone, which at that moment reported a message.

"Yeah, you better stop," Frank asserted though anticipating more blows.

In light of her discovery, "uh-huh," she dragged, "so you say I'm not doing my work, but here you are texting you know who," she paused as she inspected the screen. Frank took the chance to escape from under her, and in doing so reflected his cover, the comforter; sheets, pillows and all as he jumped to the computer to begin a new track. Now buried under all that was not her work and, certainly, not her business, Maddie took her time reading through Frank's messages.

"Ohp, I'm about to play your favorite artist, or is it second favorite?" At this point, Frank was talking with himself for Maddie was not listening, but he did not seem to care. As she was engrossed in his business, he was enrapt of hers. The two entered silence just long enough for Frank to work up the negative emotion. "Are you kidding me, this is what's been taking you so long and why you find it necessary to turn off my music so you can *concentrate* on Stan?" Turning to face the lump on his bed, "I thought you didn't even know if you liked him, but now you're going out, and then some? You know what's worse, you're looking out for numero uno 'cause you didn't even bother to tell me, the entire time."

Rising, as if from slumber with her hair tousled, Maddie cursorily wagged a lonely finger at him, "No!, no, no, unh-unh, don't give me that or anything else. Tell me, why are you talking with this idiot?" She held up his phone, displaying the glowing screen, returning it within her view as she continued to browse through the messages, "did it occur to you that maybe I don't want you to talk to him 'cause, let me see," pausing for annoyed sarcasm, "he's an ass? Why are you talking with him anyway," she posed, raising her eyebrows and turning her head slightly, questioningly.

"It's not even like you to avoid something like this," Frank gestured toward the information window behind him.

Interjecting, "why are you talking to him," Maddie maintained her inquiry.

Lowly, dolefully with a hint of pity, "but it seems all you're concerned about is what really doesn't matter or count," Frank said. Abandoning this tactic, were it a strategy, he returned to his original tone, cogently, "we both know you and Drake are done, you barely talk about him, and when you do you have nothing even remotely close to good to say. And all I wanted to know is what's up with you and Stan, as he seems to be what's important to you, apparently."

"Damn you Frank, just tell me why you're talking to him and what you've been saying. What's going on between me and Stan is none of your business," this response from Maddie resulted in a palpable sigh from Frank. One not due to fatigue but that seemed to drain a significant amount of energy from him. "I mean so what, we talk and are hanging out 'cause he's like my best friend," Maddie was second to Frank in realizing the significance of what she said. The palpable dispirited demeanor on Frank's face, of his person, became a heart wrenching dejected stupor.

Almost inaudibly, "not my business, and 'like your best friend'," he repeated, quoting Maddie. There followed a period of silence during which Maddie, as given by her conceding nods, relented of her interrogation and made to gather her belongings in preparation to leave. Frank tried no attempts at stopping her, but as he moved to allow her room to gather her work and study material, Maddie stopped to say, "you know what, I think you're right about me and Drake. And since the two of you are so close now, you might as well tell him to never speak to me again 'cause I never want to see him. And oh, thanks for letting me use your computer but I don't think I'll be needing to do this again."

"No, I don't think you will," was Frank's retort, and as Maddie moved toward the door, opened it, Frank reproached, "what the hell is wrong with you Maddie? Did it ever occur to you that Drake and I are talking because I want another job that actually has decent pay? Have you even considered why I missed hanging out with you before your first day of school, or does our spending time together mean so little to you that you don't even think to wonder why?"

His acidulous interrogations, however rhetorical, were penetrating, and Maddie's only mode of defense was, "I don't need this stress right now, or ever. I don't need it from Drake, from school, and I certainly don't need it from you. Only one person seems to understand that."

Stan: so I'm guessing we'll talk more about camping later, but start putting together a list of things I should bring because I've never really been camping...

 Sent at 1:05 PM on Friday

Stan: I just e-mailed you some of what I have in mind. laright I've been on this thing for about an hour, so I'm going to go do something else

Sent at 1:07 PM on Friday

Stan: ok, I'll be at your place by 6:20ish, text me

~

Maddie's drive home was not usually fraught with discordance, conflict, cognitive dissonance, or the preponderance of symptoms associated with anxiety, and distress. This was especially true when she was coming from Frank's, and ordinarily her level of merriment was associated with her visits to him, correlating positively with the frequency. However, this was not the usual or ordinary circumstance within which she was used to associating with Frank, and as such the composition of her character was smarting. Consequently, supervening upon the situation was her desire to speak with somebody immediately. Supposedly, it is natural to want to talk with someone after such emotional disquiet, and Maddie was somewhat pleasantly surprised to find her father's automobile parked in the usual way on the driveway as she pulled into it.

Her approach and entrance into the house was nothing out of her ordinary. However, her conspicuous course instead of passive avoidance, as was usual, caught her father's attention within a minute of his knowledge on her presence. Directing his attention to her instead of regarding his magazine, he gave a look of concern and wonder that may best be described as perplexed. "What's up," he asked.

What he saw of her mien was the residual artifacts of the emotional fallout between what had transpired with Frank and her. Because she had sat down with the interest of talking with her father about something completely different, yet somehow related, she answered his question listlessly, "nothing, just a fight with Frank."

Quizzically, "and when has it ever been bad enough that you need to talk to me? Anything serious?" Coldly staring back at him, her tacit response was implying. "I meant, anything serious I should know about?" When she did not respond, he continued, "look, if you need to talk, as you can see I'm still here. When you have something to say, and do so in a dialogue manner where I can ask questions so I better understand what's wrong, then we can get somewhere."

"Don't pat me," she began, referring to perceived condescension, "it's a little too late to try acting like a father dad, don't you think?" Nothing, he said. The reticence that ensued was timed with the periodic turning of pages by her father. It was Maddie who finally broke the silence, "why did you and mom get divorced?" Her question seemed genuine.

"That's what you want to know, and all this…," was all he managed to say before being interrupted by Maddie.

"No," shaking her head for conviction, repeating, "no, it's not." This time there was brevity in the soundlessness, "dad, do you believe in God?"

"Maddie, what's wrong, why are yu...," he was again interrupted.

More calmly and with less emotion, "dad, just answer the question," Maddie urged.

"Well I," putting aside the magazine and resting his elbows on his knees, Maddie's father cleared the imaginary cobwebs from his lips and cheeks by wiping his hand across and under his nose. "Mind you there is a God, it's your mother who doesn't believe," he paused, searching her face and his mind, simultaneously, for the right words. "It's just, I don't know that I like all the rules, laws, and Commandments." His hands, together, were rubbing, "but the thing you have to remember is that God forgives, right, and so that means…"

Seemingly disinterested, "do you think Gramps believes in God," Maddie repositioned.

"Your grandpa, oh yeah he believes in God, and not just, he loves God, and you wouldn't believe how much that man prays for us. For you and the rest of our family. It's quite sad actually that he hasn't been able to go home from the hospital because he would be the perfect person for you to talk to," was his answer.

"I've been praying for him, and I really believe he'll get better," she admitted.

Amazed, "I'm glad to hear that, I'm sure he would be too and I'm sure he will Mad," referring to his daughter in what approximated a term of endearment.

The dialogue was beginning to sound more like conversation, "I think I'm gonna go see him this Sunday. The last time I was there, all he managed to squeeze out was lovey-dovey stuff," she smiled as her eyes burned, beginning to well with tears. Avoiding the ensuing emotion, she posed, "and what about Grams?"

Amused, "are you kidding, have you never heard a word she's said to you, especially, I mean the woman is the epitome of Christianity," he replied.

"You really believe that," asking genuinely, "you really think that she's right when she says all those things about what I'll become because of the clothes I wear, and, and the way I talk and about the people I hang out with?" Maddie was unfinished, but paused for her father's response.

"Well, yes and no, I mean, I don't know. I think that that's the way she is and how she knows, maybe even likes or wants to be a Christian. The only...," his unfinished responses were nothing new in the dialogue.

Mystified, Maddie expressed how she felt. "Really dad, 'cause I'm damn sure there are better ways to be a Christian, and I'm not saying I know exactly what those ways are or even close to it, but don't you think that since God is a loving God that Christians," nauseatingly, "should be too. I mean, the way she talks with people sometimes makes me so...," it was the first time she was interrupted by her father.

"Maddie, is this why you wanted to talk, so you can tell me how much your grandmother displeases you, now that her husband isn't do…," Maddie's father was beginning to become annoyed at his daughter.

"No, dad. I think that if people were more honest about these things then we all would have to say, or at least admit that the way that woman conducts herself sometimes, is just…." To Maddie's surprise, her father raised his voice to overpower hers, something that had not happened in the most recent years of her life.

"You stop it, right now young lady. She, your grandmother is in pain as much as your grandfather and you're going to sit here and insult her as if she were the girl you didn't like in school?" Livid, and now standing, he continued, "I don't want to hear you talking about your grandmother like that again, or anybody else in this family."

Rising to leave, "whatever," was Maddie's response.

"And who the hell puts these ideas into your head? First you begin to wear these skimpy clothes, shop at Victoria's Secret, and in your *grandmother's* words, like you're grown. And then you got piercings and tattoos, now you're disrespecting your own family? What's next Maddie, you're going to get pregnant?" She did not make any attempts to counter his words, recriminate, or stop him. Thus, he continued, "who is that boy you've been seeing, and why do you feel the need to keep your time together to the car and in the driveway? Answer me Maddie." Waiting for an answer that was not coming, "you've never felt the need to keep the boys you were seeing away, and I've actually not minded that, but now you are hiding in the car when you see each other?" The end to his tirade was given by the noiseless click as her bedroom door closed.

~

Successfully having beautified herself, Maddie donned the remainder of her outfit, a pair of heels. Clicking her way about the hall and stopping at the mirror in it to review her image, Maddie took notice of her father who was still in the large living room.

"And where are you going," he asked.

Sighing, "I'm going out for dinner, and *that* boy is picking me up. I'll probably be back around ten or eleven, so please don't lock the door, I'll do it." Her pause was in consideration of what she would say next. "Dad, I'm telling you this because I think it's the right thing to do, and I guess I'm sorry about earlier," again pausing, "I just don't want there to be any stress, for you, for me, or between us. It's really not good."

Dumbfounded, Maddie's father did manage to ask, "when are you guys leaving?" As if cued, rang did the doorbell.

~

Well on their way to the home of the original Buffalo chicken wings, Stan found it within humor to ask, "wow, are you sure this isn't a date, 'cause you look good."

"What, no. This isn't a date," assured Maddie, yet unsure, "is it?"

"Maddie, I was kidding," smirked Stan. She breathed a smile, and he continued, "your dad seemed nice. What did you tell him about me?" When she did not acknowledge his query, he explored, "everything alright, you don't seem as, you know, you?"

"Yeah, I mean my dad and I got into a spirited conversation," she paused, "for the first time in a long time, and I feel like he was right about some things." Turning to look at Stan, "and the weird thing is that I feel I was right about some things too. Now I don't know if I'm angry with him or myself for not having apologized, and the thing is I don't think either of us was wrong."

Sympathetic, "well, family is complicated, and I don't want to pry into family matters but if you want to talk, I'm listening," Stan said.

Simpering, "no." Capitulating, "well, I didn't really tell him anything about you, but he assumed we were seeing each other." Only Stan chuckled as Maddie continued, "saying how we hide in the car and stuff," she added, to which he laughed aloud.

"You know, it's funny 'cause my mom kind of did the same thing the other day," Stan added, "she thought we were dating."

"Yeah, she, my dad, and it even seems like Frank thinks there's something going on between us," Maddie seemed more pensive than her comment suggested.

"Why does everybody think we're involved," Stan's question almost seemed genuine.

"I don't know that *everyone* thinks that, but," simpering once again, "maybe we should," and sobering as she responded. Stan laughed as he understood her reply to be jocular. The remainder of their conversation in transit was focused on that day's happenings with respect to Maddie. She did not seem to need any comforting, but Stan's attempts at commiseration were not entirely abortive.

Arriving at the restaurant little less than an hour after beginning their drive, the two were seated and served relatively quickly; there were more people to seat and serve on Fridays and Saturdays, but Stan, it seemed, was a regular. The interaction between the two was not unlike a date. Singularly concerned with each other, their exchanges covered a gamut of personal information and addressed such things as favorite artists, books, television shows, and magazines. Maddie, in particular, mentioned a thing, and another, on her family, but often maintained a self-ish discourse. And on her plans about her life and schooling, urged, "I'll thank you to remind me to tell you more about that later." Similarly, with

Stan, he expressed his ambitions about being a cardiologist, his gratefulness at the quality of education he was "blessed" to receive at their school, and his pleasure about the time they were, together, spending. However, their conversation was not without a healthy sprinkling of dares and bravado in attempts of food choices and selections that invariably resulted in bright- or bleary-eyed laughter, whether mutual or at the expense of one another, and merriment.

Having spent little more than an hour dining, their table conversation was coming to end, though this was without the knowledge of Maddie, who asked, "so what would the ideal girl that you'd want to go out with be like?"

"Well I'm already out with you, so I guess that sums it up," he chuckled, alone, to himself. Quaffing the remainder of his beverage, Stan considered Maddie's question seriously as his amused face turned to one of reflective contemplation. "Well, along with being pretty, smart, funny, and uh," as he thought, Maddie could not help but think she was the first few but not the last, "and attentive. They would also have to be authentic, you know, really know who they are and what they want, and most importantly," he raised his hand with a finger as if to make a point, but signaled to a waiter for the bill ticket.

Maddie was almost alarmed and appeared, if anything, vexed. "What, are we leaving already," she asked, and seeing Stan nod as he directed the waiter to their separate tickets, protested, "but I'm not ready to go home yet. Besides, it looks like there's going to be entertainment."

"Neither am I," Stan assured, "we're going somewhere else, and the entertainment is jazz music, you won't like it," he further asserted.

"So what," Maddie's expression began to soften, "we're going to another finger-food restaurant," she quipped.

"No," Stan began, but seeing her inquisitive eyes, added, "we're going somewhere else, and it's a surprise. I really think you'll like it," adding, "after all, seems like you liked it here." Conceding, if reluctantly, she agreed with her body as it rose out of her seat, and as she began to gather her purse, Stan remembered, "have I told you how amazing you look?"

Maddie's response, "I do look good, I mean I better," was, perhaps, the extent of her narcissism, especially as she quietly added, "why am I so awesome?" However, her smile was not alone. "So," she began to remind him, "most importantly?"

Stan must have been overly pleased with their dining experience for he, upon exiting the building and breathing in the cool, dry air of the lit night, took a few quick steps and jumped in the air as he attempted to touch his heels. He partially succeeded as he had managed to touch one heel to the mid-sole of his shoe. Landing, he turned abruptly to face Maddie who was walking in his direction. As she neared him, he positioned himself directly in front of her and began to step backwards, giving a response after being reminded, though never having forgotten. "The most important thing is that they be my friend, then my best friend, then my best, best friend." His shallow smile was hidden in the dark, "that's what the ideal girl I would date would be like," he concluded as he turned, unlocking his car, and prepared for their next destination.

~~

It was during their retour from their final destination of the night that Maddie remarked at the dangerously-close to out-of-control car that narrowly missed hitting a tree as its tires plowed the dirt around it. "Wow, that person's a crazy driver, they almost hit the tree in front of that nursing home," she pointed out.

"What," insincerely, "that would have been you," Stan said, quickly, in a joking manner. He had taken them to SoftSpot, and true to his intuition Maddie had liked the surprise. Wanting to continue but stopping herself, she had unnecessarily reminded Stan of their appointment for the following day.

Maddie laughed in return, "yeah, maybe the speed, but I'd never be so reckless as to almost hit a tree." She turned to look at Stan as she said, "you know, we make a good Two," referring to their earlier delectations.

"Yeah, we do," Stan responded. After a little while, "but you could have been better on our first play, but I know it was your first…"

"Yeah, right," Maddie teased, "you could've helped by telling me they were on our backs. Besides you almost lost it for us during the last play, and who came to the rescue," she asked with a tone of raillery, "me."

Theirs was a night of merriment and this time they both knew it would have to end, and soon. They were but minutes from Maddie's house when Maddie opened and began looking into the glove box of Stan's car. "What are you doing," Stan asked as he observed her, "you can't just go into other people's stuff." He did not seem serious.

"What, OK," Maddie taunted as she continued, "I've been in this car like three-hundred times," exaggerating.

Feigning ignorance, "really?" Stan recalled, "'cause you've been in this car like *three* times."

Almost accusatorily, "what is this," Maddie asked as she held up a book she found in the glove box.

Taken aback, Stan answered, "Maddie, that's a Bible," his head and neck extended.

"I know what it is, Stan, I meant, do you always have it in your car," she asked, adding, "duh."

"No," he began, riding the remainder of their good-time wave, he joked, "sometimes I actually take it out and read it."

Maddie nodded in response as she turned on the cabin light and began to read the book. She said little from that point on, and Stan seemed content at letting her read even as the light in the cabin made driving slightly difficult. A few minutes passed before she looked up to see that they were in her neighborhood, and she sighed quietly to herself as she read a few more lines. She looked up, again, to find that they were on her street and so she placed the Bible back in the glove box and remained still as she looked straight-ahead. She yawned as Stan drove into her driveway, and turned sideways to monitor her friend. The infectious behavior was observable in Stan moments later. Tired, though they were, neither wanted to leave, and Maddie started, "that was great. I didn't think I could have so much fun and not be," correcting, "under the circumstances." She seemed to melt in her seat as she relaxed completely and slouched back.

"For what it's worth, that was the best time I've had all year," admitted Stan.

"Aww, I'm so happy to hear that." Maddie was pleased, "probably the same here. Listen," she sat up, "I had an awesome time and just want to say thank you, but…"

"You're welcome," Stan interrupted, "but you know you were half of it." Before Maddie could respond, Stan joked, "I mean like half of what you could've been 'cause you lost us our first play, which makes you a quarter since you're half of our team."

Challenging his jest, "hey! I held my own after I knew what I was doing, and I snuck up on other players almost better than you did," Maddie reminded him.

"Actually, you're probably better than me at that because I've played that field before and I figured out where most people like to hide," Stan agreed partially. Continuing, "you remind me of an assassin the way you tip-toed around and how quiet your steps were."

"Tch-yeah, I'm more like a badass, ass-kicking assassin," Maddie's response was with confidence.

"Wow, that was a lot of ass, you sure you don't want to throw in for yourself 'an assassin who's assignments are never harassed by'," as he searched for a word, a laugh began to form on Maddie's mouth, "by assaults that may prove embarrassing?" The question was hardly serious. They both wailed with laughter.

"Yeah," descending from her hysteria, "but I need to tell you something. Something you probably won't like," Maddie seemed slightly concerned.

"I actually have something to tell you as well. What is it," Stan asked.

Placing her hair behind her ears, she smiled dryly as she said, "you know, you didn't remind me to tell you, but about school, I'm probably going to…"

"Oh, that reminds me, I forgot to tell you that I won't be in school the last couple of classes. Just something I have to do with and for my family," Stan again interrupted.

Raising her eyebrows in question, "is that all that you were going to tell me," Maddie asked.

Shaking his head, Stan formed a hollow, "no," adding, "I thought you were going. But I wanted to show you something that I made for you, well, it's about you, but it's also for you, definitely," he concluded, if a little tongue-tied.

"Oh, really, where is it," Maddie looked around as though she expected he would withdraw something, anything, from its hiding place. Seeing nothing, she again pried, "ok, what is it?"

Stan smiled, "I'm glad you're excited, but I'll show you tomorrow, it'll be a surprise." After a silent moment, he asked, "you were going to tell me something?"

"You know what, I'll tell you tomorrow, it'll be a *surprise*, trust me," Maddie assured. Immediately, she opened the door and made to step out, and with her right foot on the ground, turned back to Stan, saying, "I just need you to know that I appreciate our hanging out, and really need you to know that. See you tomorrow." Taking egress with similar immediacy, her statement was with such finality that Stan was left wondering what exactly, if anything of significance, happened. Not displeased that she was willing still to keep their appointment for the following day, he did not know whether he should be displeased with something. And he certainly did not know whether there was something, particular, with which Maddie was nettled.

As such, Stan watched her as she walked toward and into her house. Left only with his thoughts and her words, he slowly made his way out of her driveway and, it seemed, his confident knowledge of her person.

Neuf

Uneventful was the drive, scenic perhaps, but uneventful all the same. With the exception of few stops for gas, refreshments, and food alike, the trip was one long drive and Maddie steered most of it. Indeed, they had great fun for which Stan was grateful and informed Maddie. The two were aware that they may have feelings for each other, but neither pursued emotion and each rationalized. Maddie thought that she was in fact really only interested in Stan's friendship, and that any extra feelings were resultant of her emotional states which were influenced by her grandfather's condition. Stan, on the other hand, assumed he simply was in no need of a girlfriend. That he was her best of friends, regardless of how he felt, and she his only girl friend, the fact was.

They were not far from their destination when Maddie asked, "Stan, is there any sexual tension between us?"

Stan had reclined his seat during their travel and his arms were folded about his face to block the hot yellow moon. His eyes remained closed as he shook his head against his arms, "no. Why, do you think there is, do you think I'm sexy," he teased.

"I think you're handsome." When she saw him begin to loosen and remove his arms to peer at her between them, she added, "but I don't think I'm attracted to you," more to convince herself than Stan.

"Whether I'm attracted to you or not, I think you're attractive," Stan admitted.

"Thank you," was her response.

"You need hardly thank me," he murmured.

Twenty minutes would elapse before they reached the State Park, which was short, an intangible something, of marvelous. Maddie had practiced reserve and prudence by not telling Stan she did not want him driving her car much, if any, of the way, but she had become fatigued and wished Stan to drive. Breathing in the scene as they both stepped out of the green hatchback, the air outside the vehicle seemed stiflingly hot when compared to the damp-like cold of the car's interior. The two traded places, Maddie in the passenger seat, and Stan as the driver. Maddie held a map of the entire area, of the gorge, of waterfalls, rivers, roads, park and all. The "Grand Canyon of the East," as it were. She began searching for their campground as she simultaneously instructed Stan on how to navigate the entrance to the park and make way through the somewhat confusing and serpentine roads. The car was weighed down by camping equipment such as the tent materials, a portable stove, clothes, sleeping bags and pillows, shoes and boots, buckets and, two bikes. As Stan drove, the car hummed to Maddie's music.

"Can we change this Gaga crap," Stan asked, referring to Maddie's music choice.

"Actually, it's Nicki Minaj," Maddie corrected, but upon seeing his indifference, "fine, but I don't think you're going to like this," she ejected the compact disc. "The radio's not too good out here."

With authenticity, "don't you have another CD we can listen to," Stan posed.

"Um, yeah, I like this one actually," Maddie brought out another compact disk which she inserted into the compact disc slot, aglow with a faint light.

The music had played for some time before Maddie began to explain the significance of the mixed album, its sentimental value for her as it was her grandfather's. Her Gramps, she explained, had been deployed sometime between 1965 and 1968, the more involved years of the Vietnam war for American troops. Something about an Offensive. Help, Yellow Submarine, and All You Need is Love, to name a few, played in the background as she spoke. "He was a gunman, and even though he didn't see much, it was enough to make him drink." The popping sound of opened can bottles, helicopters, and other sounds were all reminiscent cues that could remind him of "having to shoot at suspect Vietnamese, whether harmless citizens or dangerous 'charlies'." It was no thing of wonder that her grandfather had led a troubled lifestyle after the war, and his drinking and heavy smoking were but a couple of the physical manifestations of his trauma. She detailed the significance of his life on hers, smiling, "but he gave all that up when I was born." She relayed her grandfather's putting away of his old habits, the support he gave her parents, and how he never made her feel judged. Always defending her, against her grandmother even.

Stan did not know what to say, but he listened as his lips mouthed the words, "because that's what love is, or at least what it looks like."

With her knees level with her head, and her feet resting on the inside of the passenger door, Maddie had leaned back in her seat and her shoulder rested on the center console. With the small map blanketing her midsection, when she was not reading it to inform Stan's turns, her head faced it and the door so that it seemed when she talked her audience was the window. She began to tear, and though she would not have cared to wipe her eyes, Stan could hardly see her face. However, it was not necessary he see her face as he could hear the sad regret in her voice, the emotion as she continued. "I wish I had gone fishing with him like we used to before I started school, but every time I'm not going to school it's like I have to work," her sigh served as a pause, "it's not like I'm making that much money but if I could buy time," she admitted, more to the window than to Stan. "Now I'm taking these classes over the summer instead of spending more time with him and my family." Turning to Stan, "and you know that vent in the back of class," Stan nodded a response to her question, "it always reminds me of the machines and computers in his room."

It was not long before Stan added to the conversation, "Maddie, I'm sure you already know, but he loves you. You love him as well, and the best thing you can do to help him is pray. The thing is that as much as he loves you, the source of all the love in the world comes from God, because God is love. When you think about it that way, since God is the source of love, all you can do is pray and believe he'll get better."

Sitting back up, she sighed, saying, "I know. I've been praying, but I wish this prayer thing was like paying for a caramel frappuccino. You offer up your prayer and God gives you what you want." She looked at him, "I wish it was like talking to you, you know, I say something and you say something back. It doesn't even have to be something I like. I don't like half the things you say anyway," she joked, laughing.

He smiled along with her, pleased that she prayed but delighted that she wanted prayer to be like talking with him. "Well that'd be nice, and I'm glad to hear you've been praying for him. But," a pleased look on his face as he looked to her, "God doesn't want anything from you other than your words, whether in prayer, blessings, or worship. Money is not what God wants, and having chosen Christians, all God wants is our heart, and I think it follows our mind, soul, and body," he concluded.

Though they had changed places, they seemed to maintain their positions as Maddie resumed interrogating Stan. She leaned in on the center console as if to examine his foreign psyche, "so you're saying that God chose you, but not me?"

Defiantly, "what! No, God chose you too, I mean, chooses everyone. That's why the idea that we, as humans, trying to determine whom of God's children gets to live or not and all those things we discuss in class is just crazy," Stan explained.

"Hmm, you know, this whole Christian thing is more confusing than I thought. It's definitely more complicated than I was taught and how people make it seem." Maddie had a look of resignation.

Abeyance aside, Stan contemplated a response, "well Christianity is, what I think Christianity should be is basically the one on one with God, and prayer is very implicit in it." Maddie said nothing, and so he continued, "it may seem like this is easy and a fairly straightforward idea, but I struggle to try and maintain a constancy in praying. I'm sure you've heard of the story about Jesus asking that anybody without sin throw a stone at some lady that had committed a sin, meaning that everyone is a sinner. And because of that, I don't care to judge people because no one but God can really understand the complicated pasts of others. That's why I think everyone's…"

"The same," Maddie finished what Stan began saying while simultaneously interrupting him, "I know, you've told me before." With what seemed like frustration, "but Stan, we are not the same. I mean you have to see that. I don't mean that you're a guy and I'm a girl, but I mean you are like completely different. Not just because you don't want to have sex, but because you don't even think the same way as me or anyone I know. You, you believe what you believe even when others don't or even oppose it. You tell me what you think, but it's like you don't care if I listen or not because, maybe everything is great for you, and I'm glad, but it's not so great for me. It's not that easy for me to not want to, to do the things I want to do. You know, but you'd say that you won't judge because it's not your place, and that's great. It really is, but don't say we're the same 'cause it's easy for you." Looking around as though she were seeing something worthy of attention, Maddie commanded, "stop the car."

"Stop, what, why," Stan asked, if a little confused.

"'Cause we're here, that's why," seeing that he was beginning to express his thoughts by forming words, Maddie again dictated, "Stan, don't. You're making me angry and I'm trying to be glad that we're finally here."

"Well," began Stan's retort, "you're making me angry as well. You think it's *easy* for me. I don't even know what you mean by that." As she ignored him by beginning to unpack the vehicle, he helped while addressing her, "do you think I never lie, or look out for myself? For your info those are called sins, and the reason everyone is a sinner is because we're born like that, whether it's lying, killing, cheating, disobeying, or, or sex before being married, and it's all the same to God." The two had stepped over the line between cheer and annoyance much before Stan's ultimate. With poise, "it's all the same to God's eyes Maddie. All we have to do is fight it, but the trick is to do it with God 'cause we can't do it by ourselves."

She stopped, and he continued to unload the car. Maddie's hand held a fist on her hip and she ran the other hand through her hair, pulling it back. With similar equanimity, she asserted, "it's not the same Stan." When he stopped to look at her, having heard the composure and conviction in her voice, "at least not with sex," she continued. "Last night, in your car, I read that sex ws…, sexual immorality as it said, was not like the other sins because it is a sin against yourself. I mean, I don't know that it's not the same in God's eyes, but that must mean something right?" She took a seat on the thin lip of the mouth that was the back of her car.

Without her looking at him, it seemed she trusted he would catch the question she had floated in the air above them by answering. "It means you now have to pray to yourself, and hope you'll forgive yourself," Stan chaffed, humming a laugh after he saw her smile. The scene was humble as they just as easily stepped back across the aforementioned line. "I didn't know that," admitted Stan. The silence that ensued was good for the both of them.

With unvoiced understanding, they both rose to prepare for a day full of activities. Maddie had planned that white-water rafting would begin their experience, followed by walking the trails, or "trailing" as she liked to think of it. After an early dinner-break of sorts, she hoped they could bike trails they did not explore before retiring to sit by a waterfall if there was enough sun or their tent should it be too late. Though biking was not the first activity on Maddie's itinerary, to get to the rafts they would have a long walk, and so they decided to take their bikes instead. When they were almost ready to ride, Maddie, who waited for Stan on her bike, ridiculed, "you're wearing a helmet? I'm a girl and I'm not wearing a helmet."

"What, now I can't wear a helmet 'cause I'm a guy? It's not like I'm putting a basket on the front of my bike or something. That'd be a girly thing to do." Stan's rebellion could be fully appreciated when he added, "besides, anything can happen and I don't want to have a TBI."

"Ok," Maddie sighed, rolling her eyes and, it seemed, her head at the same time. "You obviously took that too far 'cause I meant you're wearing a helmet and it's not like we're going on a trail, we're just going down to the water."

Relenting, "alright, but don't act like you didn't bring one too 'cause I saw it in the car." After he returned the helmet, by throwing it at and into the tent, and they began to pedal away, Stan posed, "so, why do you think I don't want to have sex?"

Squinting at him with a questioning face, Maddie asked, "what?" It must have been then she remembered their conversation just moments earlier, because she voiced a clear, "oh, that? I, um, well, it's not like you have, and you don't have a girlfriend. I mean, you're nineteen and the thing is you haven't even tried."

"I love how you assume things, or are you one of those people who thinks that just because you're in a relationship sex is expected? But I guess it's not difficult to come to that conclusion. Just because I haven't," Stan paused long enough for Maddie, who had shrugged him an answer, to turn and look at him, "doesn't mean I don't want to."

With the semblance of surprise, "so you do?" Maddie's question, to her shock, was filled with anxious anticipation.

Equally surprising and straightforward was Stan's response, "my decision to abstain from sex, while ostensibly religion driven, is not a way that should imply my disinterest in the act and so preclude a desire, but is simply a measure I hold to prove love in marriage."

Maddie blinked, twice, as if to process what she had heard. She seemed to process her words as well, "wow, that was very well-spoken."

"Yep, that's what I've prepared in advance for people who ask me that question," Stan began, "that's probably why I don't have a *girlfriend*," he mocked.

Semi-dumbfounded, but smiling, she looked for clarification, "so you don't think you will like sex?"

"No, I'll love it, but… hold on, I haven't thought about this one," was his answer, which she found amusing. "Being as it might that I can't give truth, for I may lie, promise, for I may fail, I hope to hold on to something which I may offer my wife once I'm married."

"I didn't know you were so eloquent," she said with badinage.

"Only when you ask the right questions," he smiled, joking in return.

They said little much more until reaching the rafts, and then kept discourse to a minimum as the roar of the waters and sounds of nature prevented any profound communication. The river was something of wonder, and the rocks that guarded and guided her were just as magnificent. Nature is almost always beautiful, even more so when her beauty is shared with another. The two were entertained by Mother Nature throughout the day, and were completely at ease with each other. Whether it was the air, the water, rocks, or trees that brought this change about is a mystery, but that they were able to abundantly enjoy life in its moments was as clear as the pellucid substance on which they rode.

~~

The hour was late, and the moon was a waxing-crescent of a button in the fabric of stars that blanketed the night sky. Cool was the air and, though a slight breeze tugged at the tent in which Maddie and Stan occupied, if one carefully listened, the sound of water rushing over rocks was audible. There had been enough time to do all they had wished, and as one good thing ended, another began. As such, even with traces of fatigue beginning to settle in, the two could be heard talking inside their tent.

Making to sit, Maddie had just returned from her car where she had placed the drawing Stan had given to her moments before. The image of the drawing comprised a simple yet elegantly framed mirror, and in front of it stood a figure with the rear portions of a head the likeness of Maddie's. "Etched" into the mirror's frame was *James 1:22-25*, and drawn across the top of the image and paralleling the upper edge of the paper were the words, *A Reflection*. She was thrilled with the drawing, thanking Stan just once, and while she said nothing but good about it, she reminded him that in high school she found that his drawings in the school paper were usually with captions. Curious as to why hers had none she asked, "you know, I notice the picture doesn't have words as usual. Was that by design?"

"No, and yes," replied Stan, "because the mirror reflects you, I thought *you* could write whatever you think it reflects about you. So, it will have caption, but you have to put it in."

Smiling briefly, "I like that, it makes it more personal," Maddie began, "it makes it more personal, which is good 'cause I sometimes didn't understand what you meant with your drawings and the captions you put with them." They shared a mutual smile. As Stan lay back, "thanks, again. I gotta tell you, I won't be in school come," Maddie tried to find her words. She saw he did not seem to be paying attention, and his gaze was skyward which she found disconcertingly familiar as it reminded her of her recent boyfriend. Changing her approach, "what are you doing before school starts in the fall?" He shrugged her his nescience. "Well, I hope to do this again, just because it seems so short, you know," though it was hardly a question.

Without looking at her, Stan responded, "I'd like that."

"And maybe not something exactly like this, but just something that allows as much fun and," avoiding his lacking gaze, "as nice. I can't believe we have to go back tomorrow, and then we have class on Tuesday, ugh, and then when school starts we'll barely have time to hang out." It seemed all the while Stan was paying her no heed as he continued to stare off into the night. "Halloween might allow some time, but I usually go to my uncle's 'cause my cousins are the ones who need someone to walk with them to trick-or-treat now. But maybe Thanksgiving could be good?" This time she asked him directly. "Are you listening to me, what," she began to ask as she crawled next to him, and looking at Stan she found what he was staring at. Or into, perhaps. She lay next to him, and a long minute passed before she stated, "I forgot how nice the sky is at night."

She seemed to have his attention for he finally commented, "yeah, it is nice. All these stars," he seemed to pause for effect, "they remind me of hearts."

"Hearts," with something like surprise. He moaned her a, "yes," to which Maddie again asked, "hearts, heart-hearts, or love-hearts?

"Heart-hearts," Stan started, "everyone has one, and everyone that has ever lived had one. Sometimes I feel like if only people remembered this one thing, that everyone has a heart, no matter how big or small, young or old, everyone." At that very short distance between her and Stan, Maddie's look at him was an ogle. "You know, almost everything that can happen to a human affects the heart, in one way or another, and the heart can affect things too."

"So you think of people as stars that have hearts," she asked.

"Well, I guess you can think about it that way. I see everyone as a walking heart," Stan said, aware that Maddie again joined him at star-gazing.

"Everyone," she asked, "including me?"

"Including you," he turned to look at her, smiling.

She smiled in kind, "you're so weird."

Stan looked away as he said, "maybe."

Maddie continued, "but I like it." Sighing happily, "I like this."

Because, to Stan, lying was immoral, he began, "I like you," to which Maddie, laying next to him, turned on her side to face him. He turned to face her, "I like how honest you are," continuing, "I like that there are more good things about you than bad, and I like that you haven't given up on figuring out who you really are." She tried to keep her focus and connection, but her rapid blinks and loss of eye contact seemed unavoidable.

When he stopped, she continued to look at him kindly, saying, "I like your modesty, and you're pretty candid too. But, I know your prudence is due to you wanting to do right by people. I think that shows what you believe in without always trying to prove it to others," rolling over onto her back, she concluded, "and I think that's awesome." Not long after, "I have something *I* want to show you," with her smile entirely in her cheeks, Maddie got up to get her phone. Having it acquired, she sat down next to Stan with the device cupped in her hands, "but, I don't think you can handle it. You're not bad enough."

"What," Stan approximated a shrill with his voice, and he rose to imitate the late Michael Jackson, "I'm big and bad." He laughed with Maddie as he twirled around.

Laughing still, "I'm pretty sure it's just 'I'm bad, I'm bad, you know it'," as she sobered, Maddie asserted, "besides you're not bad. Tell me one thing you've done that would be bad by my standards?"

Stan did not think long when he said, "okay, but I'm pretty sure this is bad by anyone's standard. I sometimes close my eyes when I'm driving." Lightly smiling, "sometimes on a straightaway, I'll just shut my eyes and let the sound and tug of the car decide if I'm between the lines."

"I don't even know what to say. That's, like, dangerous. I mean, which, ironically, is bad, but that's dangerous-bad not bad-bad." Maddie was more alarmed than amused at Stan, who mirrored her by sitting down across from Maddie with his legs crossed. Something like dejection to his face. "Ok, it's my piercing," Maddie divulged as she scrolled through the phone to find its image.

"If it's a picture of your piercing," Stan began to wonder, "why wouldn't I be able to, is it the one on your," waxing the air over the triangle formed by his legs. Maddie nodded in affirmation and, finding the picture, she reached out to hand him the phone. Stan shook his head in refusal as he gently pushed back her hand, "no, I, don't need to see it."

"Why," Maddie asked, smarting at the rejection. "It's just a picture of a piercing, besides, no one has seen it since I got it, making it kind of useless, don't you think?"

Compunctious, but with resolve, "I apologize, but um, I just don't want to think of you that way," Stan gave her a shallow smile.

Maddie sighed in reverse as she inhaled deeply, "you want to at least see my tattoo?"

"If it's a picture I can look at," Stan cautioned.

Maddie corrected, "No, not a picture, I mean the real thing." Before Stan could voice his inquiry as to its anatomical location, Maddie had turned her back to him, pulled her hair aside and unsheathed her right arm from the sleeve of her hooded sweatshirt. As she struggled against the sweatshirt with her clothed and bared arms, she held out the hem of her T-shirt, inviting Stan's help. As he reached and grabbed the lower edge of the shirt, Maddie, on her knees and sitting on her feet, asked, "can you see it?"

Sensuously, Stan raised the shirt another inch, revealing the lower regions of her lumbar vertebrae and the black delineations of letters that formed the word, "monster," he said. Then asking, "monster, what does it mean, and why would you want a tattoo that says that?"

"I got it because of one of the songs by my favorite artists. Anyway, I just wanted to share something with you, 'cause you've like shared a lot with me, so I wanted to…," Maddie hushed as Stan did not allow her finish. His left hand was stretched out to meet her knee, her back no longer to him.

"Thank you," Stan breathed, and she throated her appreciation, "but I do have a question more for you, though."

"Me too. Hmm," she was undecided on how to approach her question.

Stan, taking it to be her considering his remarks, asked his, "now, I have to admit, now that we've talked about some things," *he* did not seem to know how to pose his question either. "I wanted to know what you thought qualified as sex. You know, other than intercourse obviously, because I think some people think things like oral sex isn't sex," and, supposedly, not quite sure she understood his question for what it asked, he qualified, "I mean of course it has the word sex in it, and it would seem to imply that, but some people don't feel they lose their virginity to it, or that way."

Maddie was caught unawares with the question, but noticing he had not paid much attention to her given his discomfort in posing it, she gave her prepared response, "ok, I think those kinds of people are idiots. First of all, because whether it's oral sex or manual sex...."

She was interrupted by Stan who was not sure what she meant, "how do you mean by manual?"

To which she respond, "um, like hand-jobs and things like that." Seeing his nodded understanding, she continued, "yeah, because there is intent," to which he was not sure she was referring to philosophical matters. "I mean, isn't that why rape is what it is," she asked, and gave the answer, "because while there certainly may be intent on part of one person, there is no intent by the other?" Again, Stan was unsure if she were referring to something from class, but he did not consider asking for he was intrigued by her already-made-mind mentality, especially given that he considered her to be someone that was very uninhibited. Yet, the fact that she thought such things as oral sex to be sex, which, he imagined, he knew others did not consider as such, left him lost in the maze that was she.

If either two thought the night would continue on forever or another minute, they showed no signs of disinterest or fatigue, nor did either have tedium. To Maddie the reality of sharing such a connection with one whom she did not know as well as she perhaps would have liked was not all together new to her, but finding her level of comfort with Stan to rival even that which she shared with her close friends, Frank among them, she fought to maintain it even against the pugnacious instinct to counter him and keep her distance. Stan was also aware of the closeness with which his interaction with Maddie had become, and although he knew himself to be within a level of intimacy which he should not supersede, it was a risk he was willing to take as he considered, especially, that she deserved all the love he could afford her without neglecting himself.

Maddie wasted little time as she remembered her questions, "so what do you think of masturbating," she explored.

Stan was caught off-guard as he found difficulty in finding his words, mouthing what he thought were the starts to his answer. "Well," he began, "it's funny you ask because my friends," he smiled in a sighing manner, and as such with a hint of sarcasm as he made quotes in the air, "have asked me about that. And I'll tell you the same thing I tell them," he prepared, "I just don't do it because I never think of it, and I know some people derive pleasure from it, and," he recounted, "I mean my one friend told me it helps him go to sleep, but I just don't see it and never thought or think of it, you know," looking for assurance as he finished and hoping she would no longer broach the topic for he seemed in a way that would have one infer he were troubled by the subject, or harassed by it.

But she did not relent, "ok, yeah, but it's good for you, isn't it, I mean…"

She would have continued had not Stan interrupted, "well I'm sure you can get into the science of it but bottom line is, I just don't see myself…"

She reentered, "but when you used to." As Stan did not want to interrupt her in anyway, he gave her a quizzical look as he angled his head ever so slightly as she continued, "you must have liked it, even just a little," she placed her tongue behind her incisors as she teethed a smile.

Stan turned his head as if to give a sideways glance, but shook her a smile in that way which indicated she was not quite correct. "Well I think you're assuming I've ever masturbated, and I haven't."

As though they were taking turns, Maddie too gave him a quizzical look as she began to mouth her disbelief, "you've never masturbated?" Seeming to have more to say but stopping mid question, "before," she completed.

His answer was anything but lengthy, "no."

Maddie shook her head in disbelief, going from side to side but finally resting her look on Stan, flexing the entire left side of the muscles in her suboccipital triangle. "Wow," she dragged, laughing, "I just, it's not that I don't believe you but, I mean, I guess I should have figured that." The two sat in silence for a moment, charged with excitement. Maddie excited, but in disbelief, over Stan's reality. Stan, admittedly, was excited at her response to his situation. "I just," she tried to begin, looking at him smiling, and they both laughed. "That's crazy, but not crazy, just unbelievable," she finished, beginning another moment of silence. The two had sat in conversation for almost an hour, and naturally Stan considered the end of the conversation near, but Maddie still had a few things in mind. "Ok," Maddie seemed to be masticating Stan's points over in her mind still, "so, what do you think of Frank, about gay people I mean?"

Unsure if she were referring to just her best friend, Stan did not want to offend her or seem standoffish. And willing to share his mind all the same, Stan responded, "well," he began, not seeming to have lost his words though his thoughts were incomplete. "I don't pretend to like it and, you know, I never used to believe it was real," he admitted with his eyebrows.

Confused, "are you talking about gay people or being gay," Maddie shook her head in question.

"Oh, yeah, well I guess that's what you're asking me, right," to himself, "homosexuality, I guess. But," he seemed to have great difficulty finding his words, and then as if letting go of his uncertainty, "the truth is, like everyone else, gays are people first. Children of God, no matter what I think."

Maddie flashed Stan a suspect smile as she grabbed her phone and composed a message. "I just sent you something," she said. Stan smiled back, and as he turned to crawl to his belongings and find his, she discouraged, "no! Check it tomorrow after we get home."

Forming an incomplete V while laying in their sleeping bags, the two conversed well into the early morning hours of the next day. Their feet pointed at the corners on one side of the tent, and their heads nearly met at the other. Maddie took to her sleeping bag, making herself comfortable as she prepared for the inevitable suspension of consciousness.

Stan continued to look at her as she lay there, and finally copying her, he asked, "is it cold out here or is it just me?"

She did not respond, and after what seemed a great while, she asked, "do you think a girl and a guy can be just friends?"

Only after a long minute did he respond, answering, "I don't know. All I know is that of all the cabins we could've rented, you decided it was better we stay out here in this tent in the cold." He turned over on his side in his sleeping bag facing the side of the tent, away from her.

"Can I hold you," Maddie asked, there seemed to be no emotion in her voice.

"What, no. Only if you think the answer to your other question is yes," were his final words before entering sleep.

~~

There, somewhere in the tent was a buzzing, vibrations of which annoyed him awake. It was dark outside still, but Stan knew he had slept for at least four hours. Having dreamt, he knew from recent personal experience that something around half of the night elapsed. He began to turn over to find the source of the disturbance and felt much of Maddie's presence behind him, an arm about him. He was unsure whether to be happy or sad, glad or mad. Taking care to do so slowly, he rolled out from under her arm which, though heavy from sleep, he found delicately light. Feeling his way in the dark, he saw a light emanating from the edge and underside of Maddie's plush pillow. Intending only to stop the noise and return to his time-consuming, but necessary, behavior, he felt for the phone and grabbed it. Fumbling to find a red button, he could not avoid reading the screen, which read: Calling... Mom. Pursuant to his goal, he shut the phone off and began making his way back into his sleeping bag.

Settled and returning to slumber, the processing power behind his senses, which had earlier informed him of the caller, were powerful enough to reduce to a meaning the potential significance of the call and its urgency given the hour. He ceased trying to fall asleep and considered waking Maddie, even as he knew the result may be their having to leave immediately and drive back, on limited sleep as it were, to Buffalo.

After Stan shook Maddie awake and relayed to her what happened, he began to ready his things. Rolling up his sleeping bag and donning his sweatshirt, Stan missed the fright in Maddie's face. She too had begun gathering her belongings, but not before she tried calling her mother to find out the reason for the early-morning call. She was unable to reach her mother, or, for the matter, her father.

Although Stan did most of the heavy lifting, namely putting the bikes on their racks, Maddie was terribly efficient at preparing them for the homeward trip. Already preparing the tent to fit in the car, she extricated her keys from the tangled mess which, along with the tent, included some of her clothes and other garments. Tossing the keys to Stan, she ordered, "start it." Within fifteen-minutes they were on their way home, park authorities informed and all. She may have trusted Stan to drive but being more experienced at the high-speed driving that maintained much of their course, Maddie drove.

As Maddie drove, Stan attempted to contact Maddie's family using her phone. Succeeding on the first try, an audible, "hi hon," could be heard from the other end of the line. "Hello Mrs. Wel..., Maddie's mom," Stan answered as he looked at Maddie for something she could not give. Holding the phone out within the range of Maddie's voice, Stan activated the speaker-phone function as the voice of Maddie's mom asked, "Mad, who is this?"

"Mom, it's me, what's…," Maddie began to say.

"Hey hon, was that Frank I heard? He sounds more…," said Maddie's mom, cut off by her own daughter.

"No, mom. It's another friend, Stan. What's up, is everything alright?" Then Maddie allowed her mother respond.

"No, Mad, everything's not alright. I wanted to ask that you get here as soon as you can." There was some alarm, but not as much as would be expected given the tone of the situation.

"Is he," Maddie began but stopped, the pause allowed emotion to imbue the exchange.

"He's not…, just get here, but drive safe, you know I don't need another headache. See you soon." Maddie's mom gave her farewell.

The music they had opted to listen to the previous day had not gone to completion. As such, Yesterday, by The Beatles, beat gently in their spaces as they travelled. Stan made attempts to reassure Maddie that her grandfather was not in the poor and that, if anything, he may actually have recovered somewhat. And, that his recovery impelled his healthcare personnel to inform her family. His conjecture was hardly convincing.

Driving with great speed, Maddie may have been scatterbrain for she had many thoughts, most of them worrisome. The worry on her face was palpable, and she said nothing as Stan fought futility in consoling her. Stan may have also wanted to comment on their speed, but said nothing to that effect. Maddie began, slowly, to control herself and emotion, reigning in her thoughts, though she did not slow down. Finally, after a while, she said, "sorry we had to leave so quickly, and I know it would've been nice to sleep in until morning before packing."

"What, no, don't apologize," Stan assured, "I'd rather we left early and get you to your grampa before anything happens." Joking, "besides, I'd rather we died speeding to your grandpa than for nothing," he chuckled briefly to himself, Maddie did not even look at him. "It's ok, and like you said, we do have before school starts and the holidays we have off to hang out."

Reminded of something, "right, I forgot to ask you, what are you doing for Thanksgiving?"

"Uh, same old, dinner with the family. Why?" Stan managed to push back his seat a little, but there were a great many things stuffed into the little car that prevented his going back all the way.

"Would you like to come over for dinner," Maddie asked.

It was unlikely that Stan would have declined her offer, but not wanting to add any more stress to her situation, he answered with something more than a simple "yes." "I would love to." Maddie gave the first of three smiles she would have that day, and even then it was light.

It was miraculous that the two made the trip back in just over an hour. That is, not the timing of their return trip, but that they were not stopped and given a ticket by highway authorities. Though Stan had suggested she stop at the hospital, and allow him take a bus home, Maddie insisted she drop him off and allow him to go home and rest. Not long after entering town, Maddie reversed into her driveway, sidling her car next to Stan's. She may have sat in the car otherwise, but as there was much to unpack from her car to Stan's, she decided to help him.

Placing the last of Stan's belongings in his car, Maddie stopped to look at Stan as he closed his trunk. Standing semi-akimbo with her right hand on her hip and the left in her hair, Maddie wavered, "so, um, text me," almost as a question, "e-mail or Facebook me so we can…"

Stan gently moved toward her, taking a step to cover the breadth of space between him and her. With both his arms extended, the left through the triangle formed by Maddie's elbow, he embraced her, tight. He was affected in the way those who dealt with the mind used the word, for he was filled with emotion. "Don't worry, there's like a million ways I can contact you, not to mention physically coming to you," he began. Maddie smiled blindly, her eyes closed. Although he *wanted* to enjoy it as it lasted, "just get to your grampa," he added before finally releasing her, however reluctantly. As Maddie made her way to her car, Stan too turned to enter his. Thinking on what she had said just a moment before, he stopped and turned back to ask her, "about your Facebook, what do you have on it about me?"

Maddie had lengthened her steps in getting to her car, and partially inside the vehicle with her right foot on the floor mat, she turned to look at Stan who stood next to his car, a hand on the door, which was closed. "Oh, nothing," a heavy smile on her face, "only that you're my best friend."

Thoughtlessly, "you're not my best friend," Stan snickered.

It was, simply, heart wrenching. The entirety of Maddie's demeanor. A lot drained from her, including color and breath, and her smile dropped to a shockingly dispassionate face, bereft of emotion. With aplomb, she entered her car, closed the door as gently as was necessary to seal the cabin, and put the already-running car in drive. With such composure, it seemed that Stan was the one who had been imprudent, and Maddie the self-possessed one. However, after rolling up the incline and upon bumping onto her street, Maddie revved the car and accelerated quickly as she turned left out of the driveway. This sent many of the gravel stones travelling back in long arches. The gravelly sound that ensued was followed by the squealing protest of tire against the craggy rough of the blacktop. Only one rock hit Stan's car as the scatter of rocks oscillated in the direction opposite the movement of Maddie's car.

Stan cowered behind his elbow as she pulled away, and grimaced at a pang not altogether physical. When he spied from behind his arm, what he saw was the fiercest of looks, one that left his hands and feet cold, but not before sending chills throughout his body. Maddie's face was a svelte expression of anger, but her hand partially blocked that image from Stan's view. As she drove away, what he saw was the extension of the unnamed but prominent middle digit. Seemingly unable to move, Stan stood there, still, and the only movement on his part was his head as it regarded Maddie departing. He had hardly a thought other than the last five words he had uttered, burning and pounding a headache into the left side of his head.

Irate, Maddie had maintained self-control for as long as she could. Trying not to believe what Stan had said, she was in disbelief that he could even say, much less think it. That after everything they had done, she thought, everything she had done, he could say such a thing. In her negative disposition, as Maddie put distance between Stan and her, she saw, it seemed, that left at her home was a complete stranger.

Stan entered and sat in his car. Turning on his phone, he waited a very long minute as the phone initiated the services necessary to view a text-message. Finding Maddie's message as the only text in his inbox, he selected it, which also took a few seconds too long to load. As he read the message she had instructed he read that morning, he began to understand the extent of the affliction caused by his words. The screen read: *You're so weird, but I like it. I think you should know that you're the best guy friend I have*, From: *Maddi*. He knew that she would not answer his call, especially as she was driving, and that she most likely would not respond to his messages for at least the next few days. Knowing this, Stan wondered how he could contact her as soon as possible. Nothing seemed potentially successful. Running out of ideas and deciding to leave, Stan happened on his only recourse. He sat in Maddie's driveway for about five minutes in prayer.

That morning, joy seemed remiss of the both of them.

Dix

It had forever been November, it seemed, and the streets were white with anticipatory measures. Salt, but no snow. The air, stung with cold freshness, refused to be still as the winds blew. Below, on the ground, the only affected bodies were those of the antlike people who scurried from cars to buildings or from building to building. The trees on the Medical South, bereft of their fleshy leaves, were skeletons of dark-brown. Barely moving, they provided some kind of constant behind the change, an equable condition that allowed Stan think as clearly as he could. Celled-off from that external environment and every bit the scientist, Stan was in the laboratory on a Saturday working when many other students would have taken the day off.

Seldom did anything distract him from his work, not even the belly-aching, mind-dulling, heart-straining sensation of hunger. No, usually, he would not be staring out a window absently, daydreaming. His attention was diverted from rat-shocking and illumination, to stress the animal, to fantasizing on how best the reconciliation of his relationship with Maddie could occur. Distrait, Stan was grinding away at his chicle-latex, masticating rather than chewing. It was his duty to shock a rat from its preferred "dark-spots," four in total, and shine on it a light when it went into open spaces in the shock-box.

After a certain amount of time stressing, over a period of several days, the rat would be taken out of the shock-box, undergo surgery to remove its heart, which would then be investigated with respect to the effects such stresses had on the myocardial cells.

Remiss in doing so, Stan allowed the rat to spend too much time in its "dark-spots," and Gustav, having observed him for some time, finally voiced his frustration, "qu'est-ce que tu fais? You're letting him have too much rest, either you do it correctly or not at all." When Stan began to protest, Gustav shook his head, "you know what, just take the day off. Go home."

"Ok, since you insist," Stan smiled without conviction.

"And I do. You've been doing ok, great maybe, especially at the beginning of this year. But, you know I know you can do better than this. Thanksgiving's next week, so work through whatever you have on your mind by Monday, and get in a couple days work before turkey day, understand?"

Gustav's exhortation was taken well by Stan who bade him "goodbye." As Dr. Pfordresher exited her office, she asked about Stan as she witnessed his departure. "He's been absentminded, so I told him to go home" responded Gustav, "no, he'll be alright. I guess it must be some family stuff," answering another of his principal investigator's questions.

Walking to the bus stop, Stan pondered whether it was best he continue to send Maddie the plethora of messages he maintained and hope she would at some point, rather soon, respond out of annoyance. Or perhaps, he thought, he could have some success at calling her home phone directly. Of course there was a risk of receiving her father's anger as well, considering the father and daughter being on speaking terms. The situation would not have been so seemingly difficult had he seen her in school, certainly she could not avoid him then. After all, ignoring an e-mail, text, a call, or other forms of communication was one thing, and easily done. However, to avoid someone completely was another. But somehow she had kept her distance and he, not knowing how that was possible, was almost always on the lookout for her. A few times, he thought he saw her, and twice he followed students in the CAT and Old Main only to find that Maddie was the only girl he had not seen or investigated in the entire school.

However, unable to find her, he wondered for a long time whether she had left school completely, and worse, because of him. Having tried exhaustively for more than three months with no success, and admittedly relaxing a little, Stan was becoming desperate. And with his desperation were venturesome thoughts, none more satisfying as the realization that she had invited him to her Thanksgiving dinner. Later reminding himself that she had not rescinded his invitation to the dinner, he decided he was going to show up unannounced and leave her little choice in seeing him. He found himself clever in this regard, thinking his resolve as his best recourse.

~~

There were many guests, many of them family, in the Welsch home. The passing of a husband, a father, and a grandfather somehow strengthened the family bonds, tightening them as it did. Tragedy, somehow, seems to always bring people together. About the rooms and spaces of the house were eight adults and several children. Most people were in the living room, a spacious and embellished yet reserved and modern chamber, being entertained. Few occupied the kitchen; Maddie's mother, grandmother, and uncle. But they were hard at work, ferrying handfuls of many foods from the kitchen to the adjacent dining room. And the children, running and jumping about, and abounding with energy, numbered four.

The home of accountants may not always be so beautiful and pleasant, but having only to care for himself and his daughter, Mr. Welsch was able to afford a large and well-kept home which could be useful during holidays. And being a holiday as it was, and the dearth of snow making it all the more pleasant, the house was alive with merry people who, even amidst their mutual and recent loss, were grateful. After some had shared what, if anything as some of the children were shy, they were grateful for, Maddie expressed her gratitude. "I'm thankful that we're all here, together, again. That even though we lost Gramps, that we still have each other. I'm lucky, actually blessed to have such good parents who work really hard," referring especially to her mother's occupation as a pharmacist, "and who still love each other through me." There were two married couples, Maddie's uncle and aunt, and mother and husband. "And, I'm glad there's no snow," she concluded.

As they prepared to say grace, all around the dining table with arms connected, the beagle, first to sense someone outside, barked. Someone joked, "she wants to join in prayer." The doorbell rang and before Mr. Welsch had made his way off and out of his seat, Maddie jumped, "I'll get it."

"Maddie, you've been getting the door all day, aren't you tired," asked Maddie's mother, "let your father get it, or are you expecting somebody?"

"But everyone's here," Frank, who was in attendance, pointed out.

Maddie's response, "actually, I am expecting someone," may not have surprised anyone, but that they watched her as she went to the door would have anyone infer that their attention was not without reason. When she opened the door she saw Stan, one hand in his pocket and the other supporting a covered pie. "What are you doing here," she thought, but, "hey," she expressed.

"Hey," he echoed. "Brought your favorite," Stan added, lifting the tart pastry a little higher. His heart shivered as he showed her the pie because he, simultaneously, saw the figure that was her father, approaching. The smell of the pie seemed to overwhelm his olfactory sense, and heat from the pie suddenly seemed insufficient in warming his palm and digits.

"Come on in," welcomed Maddie's father.

As Stan was led inside by Maddie's father he was unable to say anything to Maddie, and the two said nothing to each other as they walked back to commune with the rest of her family. As they reentered the dining room area, someone asked, "well, who do we have here?" With that question began a series of inquisitions about the guest and about the relationship, and its nature, of the guest with respect to Maddie. Many questions were posed and several answers given, but few, if any, of the exchanges were between Maddie and Stan.

"Perfect," said Maddie's mother after some time when Stan uncovered what he had brought, "now we'll have four cherry pies," and the group laughed. "But, for now, why don't we let these two talk alone. You guys can take your food to your room," looking at her daughter, and smiling soberly, she added, "go on." Maddie said nothing as she rose to take to her room, but communicated her gratitude with her eyes. She led, Stan followed.

When he closed the door behind him, she was on her bed with her food next to her. Looking at him, she said nothing. Stan paused, as if unsure what to do. Looking around, he said, "I've never been in your room before."

"I guess you haven't," Maddie replied.

When he saw her disinterested, he began quickly, "I'm sorry about what I said. I'm sorry about how I made you feel, and I'm sorry for any pain I caused."

She was quiet for some time before she added, "and you're sorry that you never came." As Stan pondered what she had said, Maddie saw the lack of understanding in his face. Stan smarted as his confusion was eliminated both by his realization and her explanation. "You said there's a million ways to contact me including coming over, but you never did."

"I'm sorry," was all he managed.

As Stan was still holding his plate and beverage, "you know you can put those on the desk," Maddie offered he sit and make himself more comfortable.

When Stan set his dishes on her desk he saw her drawing, taped at the three regions where it had been torn. In addition, however, the drawing was colored in and in the mirror's framework was *2 Corinthians 1:3-5*, on the opposite side of the first and original inscription. To the left of his dish and beverage was a bible in excellent condition. As he picked up the drawing to inspect it, there, under it was a notebook. Opened to two of its pages with writings on them, it was Maddie's journal, and undated, some of it read:

I chose a little hot pink black striped dress. I went up to the guy where he stood and stood sexy. Then I awkwardly said, "Do you need to see my ID?" Great…Now I'm laughing, why am I so awkward? That is when he said no, there aren't girls that come in underage really, only guys come in wanting to get down and claim they forgot their licenses. Lame. The best way to get away with something is to act smooth. You lost it? C'mon.

After the party I went to drop Sherrie off at home as fast as I could. She had to work the next day, and so did I. But I wanted to see Drake. I was so excited. He had texted me all the way back in Wal-Mart. I was practically jumping out of my skin I was so anxious (in a good way, which my body clearly wasn't used to) it was like I drank a whole case of Diet Coke, which I would never object to. I drove home, which it's only about a ten minute drive and as soon as I got there I told him I would be ready to leave soon and he said he was on his way. Really? I have been waiting for this day for what seems like so long. Truth is, it hasn't been so long, maybe four and a half months so long. I have waited plenty of time and I know it will be worth it. I just want to be out, with a guy, why the hell do I feel so self-conscious. Besides, it's not like I don't know him, I mean it's Drake we're talking about. I was so preoccupied with thoughts of him that I lost my keys, so much for being smooth.

I put on an outfit that I was sure was perfect. Sexy enough to feel good about myself, and simple enough that he wouldn't think I tried too hard and was totally crazy. I don't want to ruin the surprise but I totally nailed it. I wore my new Victoria's Secret bra, not because it was particularly sexy but because it made me feel good. It was new and the right size, 34D, and it supported my boobs. People always want to know if it is the Miraculous Push Up because my boobs are so big and I tell them that once they are Ds you don't need them any bigger especially two cup sizes bigger, what shirt could possibly contain those puppies. I opted to wear a white tank underneath an all-over lace long sleeve tee that I had just gotten with my Jeggings and a pair of brown suede fashion boots. I brushed my teeth took out my dog and then Drake was there, at my house. God I wish someone had been there to pinch me so I knew it was real. He opened the door for me and when I got in he shut it, then walked to his side, got in and started driving.

We were headed to downtown, which don't kid yourself is nothing like you would imagine downtown anywhere to be like. We were going to his friend's band space which was housed in what I thought was a deserted warehouse. It was creepy. I thought I was about to get shot and started panicking and wondering why he brought me here. We went inside and everything was grey, except the railings that were bright yellow and reminded me of when I did safety patrol in third grade. When we went into the practice space it reeked of pot and Jon, Drake's best friend, was tanked. There were posters covering the walls and it was cluttered. The obsessive compulsive side of me was screaming to come out and clean but that was one urge that I suppressed without a second thought, besides who knows what sort of messed up things I would discover cleaning up a mess like that.
We sat and listened for awhile, and while Drake did shots of rum I refrained because I didn't want to have to be peeled off of the floor like some alcoholic in a bar. It was after midnight when we left and we went to go get oreos because I had realized that I was super hungry and my stomach was rumbling.

"Wow, I didn't think I'd ever be going shopping with a girl after midnight. Are you always this spontaneous, and open?" Drake exclaimed.

"Ummm…yes," I replied in a tone that told him he should already know that. He expressed that he didn't realize how full of energy I would be and I jokingly asked if he could handle it, knowing that if anyone could it was him. I don't know what it was about him but when he was around I seemed to lose my mind. Not that I had many inhibitions, but I did have some, and they seemed to be gone so I had to think extra hard about anything I was going to say. Then before I knew what I was saying I just blurted it out, "you know you can die of a heart attack from chronic alcohol use." Ah, so much for thinking about what I was saying. My brain is the one that had to process the words and I didn't even know it was coming. Oh, maybe since I didn't actually think about it, it just came out as a garbled mess. Nope. Of course not, Drake's laugh confirmed that yes, I had just really said that.

"Oh. My. God. I didn't mean to say that. It just came out." Fuck. "It's all good," he said, "It's funny that you think that. I haven't ever heard that one before." I proceeded to explain to him that I didn't think that. A friend of mine had put it in my head and I showed him the angiogram of a patient who had a CABG that Stan gave me. He was still laughing and if I still felt stupid it didn't matter because I started laughing along, "That's going to be me! If I keep eating these oreos."

"Yeah, wow. That is pretty intense." Bzzz Bzzz. His phone was ringing; it was Jon, the wasted one. He was drunk and bored and lonely and wanted us to stop over at his house. What is the worst that can happen? Famous last lines of a fool.

Jon was out of his right mind. He was pacing and talking about star signs and records. He was stressing me out. I kept saying that we should go and he should get some rest, but he wanted us to stay. He kept coming and going in and out of the room, "Does the air seem clean? I have an air purifier." Weird. Finally after what seemed like an eternity he sat down. And as long as he wasn't pacing back and forth in front of me I guess I can deal. He started talking about his furniture, how it was from 1926, he got it because it was red and matched his walls. The same reason he had a giant Canadian flag on the wall that faced north. I had made the mistake of asking him earlier in the night if he was, in fact, Canadian. He said no, I'm American. So are Canadians. I thought to myself but that was just a technicality and I didn't feel like getting into it at the moment. For awhile we sat and chatted. Finally the true reason for Jon's drunkenness was revealed. He got dumped just like I had dumped Drake. Only then did I realize that maybe he was returning him the favor from when I had dumped him. Which one of them was handling the situation better. Probably him. He was talking about his ex and I said "So basically, she is a total bitch?" The answer yes, but she was hot. Hot or not, still a bitch I told him. And both boys were taken aback at my vulgar language.

While we were sitting there he started talking about the artwork hanging behind us and how he meticulously hung them each precisely the same amount of distance from the window in the middle. I blurted out, as I have a tendency to do, "Are you OCD?" He just stared at me, so did Drake. He responded, "Well I guess I am a little bit. How did you know?" I explained to him that I knew because I was slightly OCD and that was the reason that I was bothered that he didn't understand the technicalities about being American as all people that reside in North, South, and Central America are all Americans, and that there was a nickel on his floor and a dust bunny in the corner and the light on one side of the room was brighter than the other side. I took a deep breath and thought that they surely thought I was crazy. Drake just put his arm around me and said "Are you okay?" and though I clearly wasn't I just nodded my head and Jon just nodded "I see what you mean." I needed to leave the room before I had a total meltdown. I went to the bathroom. It was all purple. Weird. That's just weird. When I came out of the bathroom Jon was standing in the hallway outside the door. Creepy. Why are drunk people so odd. Can't they just act normal except laugh a little more? That would be so much more tolerable. He wanted to let me know that he was going to bed, but since he was drunk he was a little paranoid and wanted us to stay. Great, now I'm going to be sitting in someone else's house while they are asleep. I don't know this kid. For all he knows I'm an axe murderer. Clearly I'm not, since I have nowhere to hide an axe.

Drake and I agreed to stay for a couple hours and that we would let him know when we were leaving. He was seriously afraid we were going to peace out and leave him vulnerable.

After awhile Drake says to me, "So what do you think we should do while he's asleep?"
Great, back to square one. I suppose it was silly to even in the first place to think that he wasn't going to try anything, that we were just going to have a good night. Actually, I'm probably as guilty as he was, after all I was there. Had I thought it through, I probably would

have to admit it. He asked me "Are you going to do anything I dare?"

"Well, no. I'm not." I felt so stupid for thinking anything else other than what I knew he was thinking, but at that point, all I wanted to do was leave. To get out of there. I just felt so weak, like I had led myself into that situation even when I knew the not surprisingly inevitable outcome of being alone with a guy in a house.

"Exactly, I knew you wouldn't, yet here you are. Here we are." Wow did I feel stupid. I couldn't help but look down, I was expecting to see his hands begin to route to me, but he didn't even move. Like he was afraid to, or waiting for the right moment.

Why do these things happen to me? I must point out that going into any situation, even situations like these, I have no intentions. Things just seem to go one way or another. If I did happen to have intentions, I am thinking that they would guarantee the opposite outcome of what now seemed inevitable. However, who am I to decide what should happen before I even know my options. Now I shouldn't have to explain that desire leads to certain things: kissing, and kissing leads to touching, and touching leads to intercourse, unless of course you have incredible self-control which as you may have noticed: I do not. But let's not make this awkward.
After sitting awhile, and talking, and letting Drake get nowhere, we decide we have protected Jon long enough, after all I do have to work in the morning, so does Drake. I felt like such a hypocrite, I mean I feel like such a hypocrite because I knew I didn't want anything to happen, yet the intent was there and we were on a couch. Maybe we shouldn't actually have woken up Jon,

*who knew what will happen, he was wrecked. But we did
tell him we would let him know when we were leaving.
He emerged into the living room wearing a white v-neck
t-shirt and black sweats. He looked comfortable; I
wished I was wearing sweat pants. As the three of us
are talking, I just wanted to leave to get out, trying to be
as smooth as possible, sneak over and grab the door
handle and open it before anything else happened.
Phew, I didn't think that Jon noticed, as if that wasn't
awkward enough already.*

*They ended up talking for another five minutes or so, it
was already late enough why was it that he is 22 and
didn't just want to chill out? He was just trying to be
generous I'm sure. I was in la la land right then, my
attention only went back to the conversation when I
heard, "So did you two have sex?" Drake just started
laughing, and what a few moments before was my lips,
was now a gaping hole; so awkward. I was so disgusted
at the both of them, pretty sure they had planned that.
Our reactions must have been an obvious no because he
turned his attention to Drake and I think that what he
said was something disapproving or just stupid. I was so
out of it, I just started talking, big surprise, huh? I told
him to go screw himself, that all I wanted was a fun
night and that they sucked. Out of it or not, that is totally
something I would say. "What?" he inquired. "I don't
know. It's not like I thought it through before I said it.
We could have figured out something else to do." What
was I saying? I wanted Drake to myself. I'm totally
going to hell for this.*

*"Yes, it seems as though that is the case." I heard myself
saying. Where does this kid get his energy, I'm so tired I
feel like I'm witnessing the conversation from outside of
my own body, so I just went outside to get fresh air and
wait for them to come out. But of course, tried to*

*eavesdrop on their conversation, because it just
wouldn't be me to mind my own business. I couldn't
hear anything, and then finally I heard them coming.
Jon was again talking and I was responding with barely
sufficient replies: uh-huh, okay, and yep. "Why are you
so shy?" he asked.*

*"This is true. Bye Maddie. Nice to meet you. See you
soon?" and finally the car pulled away.
Before I knew it I was back home and Drake was trying
to kiss me goodnight again. I went inside and changed.
I was asleep within five minutes.*

*Waking up this morning was unpleasant because
normally waking up for work is unpleasant but mainly
because the magnitude of what I had done was sinking
in. It was like having a hangover with no alcohol or a
sundae with no whipped cream and cherry. I almost had
sex with Drake after four months we broke up. With all
that's happened, shouldn't I still be sitting on my couch
watching Sex in the City and eating ice cream bawling
my eyes out? Guess not. I don't know what the hell is
right or wrong, I definitely don't know what's wrong
with me. It's so stupid, all I want is for Stan to
apologize, in person, and we go back to being friends
again. Not like nothing ever happened, but at least back
to talking and everything. That's not too much to ask
God, and maybe I will. It's just so stupid how he hasn't
figured to come over, and it's stupid that I don't just call
him, but I don't want to. Now all I have is this stupid
bible which I thought I'd read, but I don't even
understand half of it or where to begin. We're having
family over in a few weeks and I still don't have it
together. School sucks and I don't have any time to make
friends there, and Frank and I don't really talk about
anything anymore. We just talk, about nothing. I want to*

scream, but I feel like no one will hear me. I just, don't even know.
What the fuck am I doing with my life? I don't even know.

"So, how are you," Stan asked.

"How are you," Maddie threw back.

"I'm fine, I'm ok," Stan looked at his hands as he sat at her desk. Genuinely, "where have you been? I mean, I've been looking everywhere for you and not once did I see you, it's like you disappeared."

"That's 'cause I'm at UB now. I'm sorry I didn't tell you, but you know I tried. Every time I'd try to tell you, you'd interrupt or make me angry. Sometimes you didn't even pay attention and you'd basically make me forget, so technically it's your fault." Maddie smiled lightly, "you looked for me," she asked.

"I looked for you," Stan replied.

"Everywhere," Maddie continued.

"Everywhere," Stan repeated.

"Wow, I can't believe you did that," Maddie shook her head, adding with her eyes her slight disbelief.

"I did," Stan affirmed and Maddie smiled, and he along with her. "So how is it, what has happened with you lately? You seem different."

"You mean before or after you acted like a jerk," Maddie asked without emotion.

"I'm sorry," Stan again apologized.

"It's ok, it's probably a good thing that happened," and with a spark to her eyes, "probably a good thing you were so *honest*," she mocked lightly. Maddie began to recount the story of what happened after she had experienced such emotional upheaval, and how it was further compounded by her grandfather's death that night. "I was crying so much, and I don't even know where the tears came from, but before I stepped out to leave he said 'we do what we know, what we know, and that is why we must learn'." The quiescence that followed was just as well, for Stan knew, without her having to say it, that those were the last words she had heard from her grandfather. As Maddie began to tear, Stan could not help but feel some of the same emotions. It was just genuine sadness and hurt that would not go away because nothing could fix it. It had been one thing to argue the permanentness and irreversibility of death in class, where everyone was in the relative with emotional distress, but because of her, they both soundly knew death was not something one could change.

"I still don't even know what that means but I started reading the bible because of him," to which Stan was surprised but said nothing, allowing her to continue, "and I think I'm starting to understand what you meant by God being love and the source of it. Because God is love, and I read that in first John four something," again

Stan said nothing, though he found her recall amazing, "if we're really Christians we should show that love according to what the bible says. And that to me means that we don't *get* to choose who we love. That means, even though I'm glad that you came today…"

"I'm glad I came too," Stan interrupted.

"I don't think you had a choice, because if you're really a Christian then you love me. You have to," Maddie asserted.

"And I do love you," Stan confirmed.

"And I love you too." After a quick pause, Maddie clarified, "but not like that, you know what I mean."

"I know," was Stan's terse reply.

Maddie continued to recount what had transpired after her grandfather's death. Detailing how, later that night, she was set to folding her clothes, a garment at a time. Slowly, she had cleared off the queen-size mattress she could barely remember getting. Into drawers went some of her articles, onto hangers went others, the delicates had been carefully tucked into their places, yet still, others had been thrown into her dirty laundry hamper. At a pace of her choice, slow, she had cleared off her bed while thinking of the novel face that was all too familiar. Stan had come, seemingly, out of nowhere into her life and taking nothing as his own, had actually given her something. But what it was, she did not know. She had continued impartial tears which were ambivalent; were they for the pain she experienced in losing her grandfather or were they exacerbated by the experience she had just before his death? The tears had continued and though she had wanted to stop, no thing she could think of could console her. She had not been confused but she was surely not in the know, of herself that was. She had told him the truth, a truth she had supposed needed be told. Most of those truths had been withheld from even her best friend, Frank, and as she admitted, from her father as well for fear of crying before either two. But the cutting truth was that she hated having to sleep in her bed, she admitted, which had almost been completely cleared that night. She had wanted her comforters and its softness to do just one thing, softly comfort her.

She admitted to thinking of Stan that night, and hating herself for it. She had disliked wanting him to be with her in a way that was differently new, for the purpose of comfort and as a friend, however brief, and nothing less nor more. Never having wanted or, for her moment, needing something as such and as much before, she was livid. For she had felt in a way like a child whose parents took something of joy from her, and causing her some discomfort or distress, were the source of comfort as well. And so, having had most of her mattress cleared, Maddie had climbed into the bed which had served for years as her intermediary between closet and body, with two thoughts and actions to accompany. Maddie had entertained the thought of rain. Its drumming on her window, and the general feel of heaviness in the air had always been a source of comfort to her. The fallacy, however pathetic, along with the thought of having her friend near, although she had known very well she was unwilling to respond to any of his messages and so prolong the time before their next interaction, she informed, had been what she thought as the perfect scenario to end that night. But having had neither, she admitted to having wept and slept.

It would be twenty minutes later, almost half an hour after the two were excused from the dining room table, that Maddie would inform Stan of her new age. "I'm twenty now."

He smiled, "congrats," yet apologetically, "I'm sorry I missed your birthday." She said nothing but smiled to herself as she sat still, but picking at her nails, cross-legged on her bed. Stan was still at her desk, "why *are* there so many cherry pies?"

"Obviously because it's my favorite, was my grandpa's favorite, and my family can't count," she smiled, to which they both laughed. "No, my uncle owns a bakery and makes the best pies, so every holiday he brings a cherry pie for my Gramps and I, one for the others, and one for the kids. And since you brought a pie, I may actually get one all to myself."

Before Stan could tell Maddie he would have to leave, and soon, to make the dinner his family was having during that holiday, Maddie's mother knocked on her door. "Alright you two, are you coming out anytime soon?" Before Maddie could answer, "are you ok hon," Maddie's mother further inquired, more seriously the second time.

"I'm fine mom, we'll be out in a second," Maddie assured.

"Ok, your aunt wants to play a game and your dad doesn't know where the cards are. He says you do," her voice trailed off as if she were walking away from the door.

"I didn't know you were Chinese," Stan stated, almost as a question.

"I'm not, well, my grandparents are Japanese," with some emotion, "I mean, my Grams is Japanese, and so was Gramps."

"That's cool. You know, I can see it a little now." Stan was reluctant to say, "Maddie, I gotta go."

"I know. When you get there will you text me?"

"No," he responded matter-of-factly.

"What, why?" Her inquiry was genuine, on the border of buffeted pride and annoyance tempered with interest.

"'Cause I will be celebrating with my family, duh," he teethed.

"Well, I mean when you get a chance, of course," she waited for his response.

"Of course, when I get a chance."

With her body language completely changed, a relaxed shoulder, forward chest, and elevated nose, she added, dragging, "good, 'cause *I* want you to know that I care about you, because…"

"Because you're my best friend," Stan interrupted, simultaneously finishing her sentence.

"Because I'm your best friend," she smiled. "And *I* know what that means," she quipped, inconspicuously checking his reactions, "the question is do you," she asked but without that interrogative, characteristic rise in pitch.

"Of course I know what that means," Stan responded quietly, adding, "and I'm glad." There was a weak but firm teeth-less smile to his lips, but more, his face.

Maddie, teeming with joy, posed, "then I think we should pray." To this Stan was surprised and responded with a blank blink and a broader smile.

"Pray for," he asked, unsure what exactly she wanted to pray for. Perhaps, he suspected, she wanted to feel right in and with the renewed relationship, considering the influence of God in her, in their lives.

"Well," she began, "I want to go to school for nursing and you want to be a cardiac surgeon, so I think we should pray for that, right?" An inquiry she already formed a response to.

"Absolutely," he responded, again surprised but hiding it, "but I want to be a *cardiologist*, and we should pray that you become a cardiologist with me," he added. To this Maddie shook her head in disagreement as she formed a dry smile.

"No, I don't like blood and all that stuff," Maddie opposed, her face wry with distaste.

"Ok," Stan closed his eyes as he waited for Maddie to pray, and Maddie followed by closing hers as well. However, when Maddie did not begin, Stan started, "In Jesus' name." Maddie opened her eyes and stared at him, smiled and reached out, grabbing his hands.

About the Author

Price Obot is a student of Psychology and Biology at a SUNY academic institution. While Christiamity is not his first work, it may do well to be received as such. He intends to pursue research and medicine upon graduation from his undergraduate studies.